D0200383

PEACE TALKS

Tim Finch

PEACE TALKS

Europa
editions

Europa Editions
214 West 29th Street
New York, N.Y. 10001
www.europaeditions.com
info@europaeditions.com

Library of Congress Cataloging in Publication Data is available
ISBN 978-1-60945-616-0

Finch, Tim
Peace Talks

Book design by Emanuele Ragnisco
www.mekkanografici.com

Cover image: © Cultura RM / Alamy Stock Photo

Prepress by Grafica Punto Print – Rome

Printed in USA

For Claudia

Ich bin der Welt abhanden gekommen,
mit der ich sonst viele Zeit verdorben,
sie hat so lange nichts von mir vernommen,
sie mag wohl glauben, ich sei gestorben!
Es ist mir auch gar nichts daran gelegen,
ob sie mich für gestorben hält,
ich kann auch gar nichts sagen dagegen,
denn wirklich bin ich gestorben der Welt.
Ich bin gestorben dem Weltgetümmel, und ruh' in einem stillen Gebiet!
Ich leb' allein in meinem Himmel,
In meinem Lieben, in meinem Lied!

I am lost to the world,
with which I used to waste much time;
it has for so long known nothing of me,
it may well believe that I am dead.
Nor am I at all concerned
if it should think that I am dead.
Nor can I deny it,
for truly I am dead to the world.
I am dead to the world's tumult
and rest in a quiet realm!
I live alone in my heaven,
in my love, in my song.

Friedrich Rückert
"Ich bin der Welt abhanden gekommen"
translated by Richard Stokes

DISLOCATION

F irst thing, every second morning, a group of us walk the same three-mile circuit. It is scrupulously signposted and graded—just so—as "moderate": the more strenuous sections offset by longer, leisurely ones.

At the meeting point, there is always a lot of faff with laces and fleeces and walking poles and energy bars. But the moment we set off across the snowfield behind the hotel any lingering irritation is dispelled. That sound—the crunch of snow boot through snow crust—crystallises the exhilaration we all feel at being out in the impeccable cold of early morning, high in the Tyrol.

We don't walk, and negotiations never go as well, on those days—mercifully infrequent—when a white fog wipes out the world in front of one's face. Then we breakfast rather later, behind copies of the *International Herald Tribune*, *The Times*, *Frankfurter Allgemeine Zeitung*, and the rest. It was Baudelaire—I looked it up online—who railed against this "revolting aperitif that the civilised man starts his morning meal with." "War, crime, rapine, shamelessness, torture . . . a delirium of universal atrocity." The point is well made, but the word aperitif has always troubled me. At *breakfast*? If you're a Symbolist poet, I suppose.

Pace Baudelaire perhaps, some of us, some of the time, prefer a book to a newspaper, despite the problem of keeping a book open while eating. Ingenious arrangements with the salt and pepper pots, with cafetières and milk jugs and unused cutlery, never quite work. The hardback comes into its own, I find, being more prop-up-able, as it were; whereas the paperback, so handy in bed, is too lightweight for the breakfast table. As to the reading going on: you'll be pleased to hear—we are a predictable lot—that I have seen more than one edition of *The Magic Mountain* being tackled, including—I am copying and pasting again—الجبل السحري.

(It was one of my younger colleagues who pointed this out to me. I am no nearer to mastering Arabic, I'm sorry to say, which fact puts me at a disadvantage in this business, my nominal eminence in it notwithstanding. I ask myself continually: how long before I run out of road? And then what? Some variant on retirement, I suppose; once a semi-relished prospect, but now almost entirely dreaded.)

No one from either delegation eats with us or walks with us or talks with us outside of the formal sessions. They have their own floors in the hotel. They pray—separately—in rooms set aside for the purpose. A murmur of it reaches us. Just as the murmur of the bars must reach them. They take their meals in the main dining room, but in designated areas at opposite ends from each other. I am careful to wish both parties good morning, every morning, and they return the greeting respectfully.

To return to *The Magic Mountain* for a moment. At some point, bringing it up—"I couldn't help noticing . . . "—might help with the negotiator in question: little somethings like this sometimes do. Though the fact that he speaks English so beautifully, so pointedly, gives me pause. Is he signalling something through his choice of reading? And if so, what?

Such minefields, darling, I can hear you saying.

Having got into our stride across the snowfield, we have to exercise caution on a small wooden bridge, as the planks can be treacherously icy. The bridge crosses a mountain torrent, though for most of the weeks we have spent here its leaps and linns have been startlingly frozen, as if by the tap of a winter witch's wand.

And let me withdraw the "as if" straight away. That rushing water can be so astonished into stillness is surely a sign of magic at work and not the agency of ice. Though, such is the way of things, the path then takes us straight into a rectilinear stand of pines with no magic about it at all. The trees are numbered and smell of the saw shed and the timber merchant. And next we cross a tarmac road, and outside a row of modern chalets stand BMWs and Volkswagens with skis and snowboards on their roof racks.

But that is the last of that. Thereafter the walk takes us away from the glitter of the resort, into more ragged pine and fir forest, to one of the steeper, rockier climbs, until in due course we emerge above the treeline of the mountain and are rewarded with a stupendous panorama of peaks. The thin ice air scintillates our lungs and thrills our faces. The sky is a filled-in blue, the only powder in the wash the dissolving evidence of an airliner at its most ethereal.

"Chief," someone says, clapping me on the back with a big bear paw.

"Yes?" I say.

The spell must always be broken. "Some view, isn't it?"

As I say.

My ever presence among the walking party—I have not missed a day—does not, I trust, inhibit camaraderie. On mornings when we have been in higher spirits, I have joined in the snowball fights and taken my turn on the metal tray swiped from behind the bar by a Grade 7. My tumbling from that tray into a hollow of deep powder provoked much hilarity. Yet it is true to say that I tend not to be part of the huddles that form and disperse, that chat and laugh together, as we make our way up the mountain. I tend to hang back a bit, or stride ahead, absorbed in my own thoughts. And of course, one must be conscious to some degree of one's station, one's position, even muffled up on the mountain. A certain distance must always be maintained.

I am making you laugh, I can tell. Well, *good*, because don't think for a moment I am in low spirits, that I am lonely. Though, of course I miss *you*. Constantly.

The highest point of our walk is reached when we arrive, and rest for a few minutes, at the little chapel that stands where the marked path forks, the other route leading to the pass over the mountain and down into the next valley.

One Saturday a group of us took that path—daringly so, we thought. What would we find on the other side of the rocky crest? The top-station of a ski lift, as it turned out. With a blaring motorway-style cafeteria, palisaded by hundreds of pairs of multicoloured skis. We took the gondola down to this other resort and then had an hour-long bus journey back to our village. Most of it on dual carriageway, in heavy traffic, heavy sleet. It was a changeover day.

The chapel is a charming, rustic structure. Tucked under a rock overhang, it has an undulating tiled roof, adorned with a simple cross. Otherwise it is basically a log cabin, tastefully weathered by the seasons. Inside, there are rough wood benches, a table with a wooden cross on it and a single stained-glass window, of abstract design, a memorial to a local man who died in a car accident, aged just twenty-two. There is also a sanctuary lamp, oil-fuelled, which, as custom requires, burns constantly, eternally. Given that every evening a candle illuminates each immaculately maintained grave in the village churchyard, it is most likely that some-one—perhaps the same person—tramps up the mountain daily to tend this solitary lamp. Yet we have never seen another soul anywhere near the chapel, or indeed any boot prints other than our own on the paths towards it. Skis? someone suggests. *Langlauf* ? I, for one, prefer to believe this ever-burning lamp is the little miracle someone would have us believe.

Whatever we believe, we all take a moment to reflect. Personal matters are uppermost in our minds, but also, I trust, the importance of our mission. We can just glimpse the roof of the hotel and the conference centre from this eyrie high above the resort. I always start looking forward to breakfast at this point. And to the business of the day.

The descent, inevitably, is somewhat anticlimactic. But it was during this morning's walk down the mountain that the incident I want to tell you about occurred. Everyone was rather bored. Not just with the hike but with being here. There was a drip-drip-drip thaw in the air, but that served only to remind us of how long the talks have been going on. Going around and around the same track, starting and finishing at the same point, getting nowhere for all our exertion . . . I am labouring this, I feel.

Then, there it was. A strong rope tied to a stout branch overhanging a gully, the rocky bed of which was palliated by duvets of snow. We had not seen the rope before and could not have missed it on all the previous occasions we had passed this way. Some local children, tiring of winter pursuits, looking ahead to spring, must have rigged it up the previous evening. Lengthening evenings: there's another thing.

It was to be seized, of course: this unexpected, mildly thrilling, above all, *new* element to our early-morning consti-tutional. Instead of crossing the gully via the footbridge, we took it in turns to swing over, Tarzanstyle, across. Several of us, perhaps for courage, did so while doing the Tarzan yell.

Yoooo-oddle-oddle-ooooooooo-yoddle-oddle-oooooo.

It is a curious ululation, when you think about it: sounding more Alpine than simian, owing more to the European origins of Johnny Weissmuller—or, to be precise, Johann Peter Weißmüller (b. Szabadfalva, in the Austro-Hungarian Empire in 1904)—than to an upbringing among the apes, e.g. Cheeta (or Cheetah, Cheta, or Chita—real name Jiggs.) As you can imagine, our little adventure was the talk of the *Gaststube* this evening. And here's another nugget—also found on the Internet—that I shared with the company and which was well received: the Tarzan call was trademarked by Edgar Rice Burroughs, so every *Yoooo-oddle-oddle-ooooooooo-yoddle-oddle-ooooooo* is technically a breach of copyright.

But the point of telling you all this is what exactly? Because I made it across without incident, I'll have you know. I was rather pleased with myself, if I'm honest, though it was a traverse of no great distance, and the degree of danger in these snowy conditions was negligible. The fact was, however, there was an accident, which was quite dramatic in its way. What happened was that the penultimate swinger, so to speak (one or two did take the bridge), dislocated her shoulder in the process. Something to do with hanging on to the rope for too long and then overextending her arm as she finally leapt.

The plosive when the ball joint of the upper arm popped out of the shoulder socket was sickeningly distinct. Our colleague—Berenice, her name is—yelped in pain and then literally fell at our feet. I was among those who—there's no other way to describe it—*recoiled*. We couldn't bear her agony; how it tore through us. Our first instinct was not sympathy but disgust; a reaction that tells you something about human nature: its default to repellent selfishness. (I need hardly add that less was made of this in the *Gaststube*.)

But we also witnessed the other side of human nature, where the better angels take to their wings. (I have been rereading the Steven Pinker book out here, incidentally: as an antidote to the revolting aperitif, as it were.) The person who stepped up was Hans, a Danish rapporteur, who turned out to be trained in first aid. With just a few firm words, he had Berenice lying flat and ready for theatre. He then braced himself, right leg locked against her side, and, with a decisive heave and a sort of rolling action, plopped the arm back into place. There was some sense of oars and rowlocks about the manoeuvre: the flailing arm, a gruesome grinding for an instant, but then smooth, almost liquid, rollerball motion.

Other than an oily film of sweat on her upper lip, there was no trace of pain on Berenice's face where moments before all was pain. Indeed, one almost felt she would have been hard put to *imagine* pain, even in the far future, never mind the immediate past, such was her surging freedom from it. (Adrenaline pumping, presumably.) She had to be persuaded not to swing the recently stricken arm around her head to demonstrate how complete was its restoration. And it was with some difficulty that Hans got her to agree to immobilise the arm in a makeshift sling.

That's it; that's the whole story. It was no great drama in the scheme of things. And I am not suggesting that there is a lesson to be drawn from the incident. Berenice has been prescribed some strong anti-inflammatories, but we expect her to be in work as usual tomorrow. Otherwise it has been an uneventful day. The talks grind on. I try to keep my spirits up.

I miss you.

THE GAVEL

To start with, it was something of an embarrassment. I even sensed sniggering among younger members of the secretariat when I first used it. But now I am most attached to my gavel and relish the sharp rap of hard wood against sounding block that calls and restores proceedings to order. Certainly, the two delegations seem to respect it, and therefore me, which makes me think the idea of having a gavel came from the (very good) cultural adviser to the talks.

At other negotiations I have presided over, the element of ceremony, the air of a court of law, that the gavel evokes would not have been helpful. After all, as I am constantly stressing, I am not the prosecutor, or the counsel for the defence, or indeed the judge of proceedings, I am a *mere* facilitator—though on this occasion that "mere" was omitted from my normal suite of opening remarks, also on advice from the cultural adviser, who thought it too self-deprecatory, too archetypally English. "I am a Norwegian citizen," I reminded her. She—a Finn of Jordanian parentage—apologised. "But people often make your mistake," I laughed. She continued with her point. "Above all, they respect strength," she told me.

You can see why we employ such advisers (there are culinary and religious ones too). It is so important to create conditions in which the two negotiating parties feel as comfortable as possible.

Which brings me to the Turkish delight. When I first saw the little bowls of it in the middle of tables, alongside the hotel-branded bottles of still and sparkling mineral water, I thought it smacked of Western condescension, of the worst kind of stereotyping. Why not the usual mint imperials? I thought (though they have problematic connotations of their own, I suppose). I was wrong about the Turkish delight, however: both delegations seem to have been very pleased with it, not just taking handfuls of the sweets themselves, but offering them around—at one particularly promising moment, *to each other*.

Sadly, the deployment of Turkish delight as a peace token was short-lived. I forget exactly what went wrong, but something was said, offence was taken, and the sharing stopped. Still, both sides continue to enjoy the Turkish delight *in common*—and that is something.

I have chaired talks where if one side starts drinking the orange juice, the other side will immediately ask for apple juice, not because they particularly want apple juice—although they will probably make a show of drinking some of it—but to make the point that if we think they'll drink what the other side is drinking we have another think coming. To which the other side—"the orange juicers," as it were—respond by drinking some of the apple juice themselves, not because they particularly want it either, but to make the point that refusing to share drinks is a petty gesture to which they—"the orange *and* apple juicers," to be more precise about it—wouldn't stoop. To which the "other" other side—"the only apple juicers," so to speak—respond by not responding—i.e. by not drinking tit-for-tat orange juice—thereby making the point—to their own satisfaction at least—that having made their point they are not going to labour it.

There was an issue the other day with the blinds. Or more precisely, how much light they were letting in.

We hold our plenary sessions in the main conference room of the complex, a room that is designed to have natural light, but no view—nothing to distract us. We are sometimes troubled by the sun angling in through the skylights, however. The blinds, as you might expect in a facility as state-of-the-art as this one, are computer-controlled. They can be adjusted minutely using a mouse-type-of-thing. And thank goodness for it, for one shudders to think what a drawn-out performance it would have been if we had had to call in a maintenance man to go up a ladder and play with the cords and twizzle that long thin plastic stick to adjust the angle of the slats, as we would have had to do back in the old days, the prehistory of ten to fifteen years ago—I am thinking of the Blair/Bush years. You going on the Stop the War march in London; me staying at home. You saying I was putting my career before protesting against illegal aggression; me laughing: "Come on, darling . . . " You muttering: "Don't you *darling* me . . . "; me saying: "Okay, but if we are talking illegal aggression, let's start with Saddam Hussein, let's start with him gassing his own people . . . "

But to return to the blinds. To the light. To the dispute at hand. You can imagine the sort of photographs and videos we must view as each side seeks to demonstrate that the other is the more bestial and therefore the more impossible to negotiate with. On the day in question, one such photograph was being displayed on our screens. Let's call it: Image 1451. (The number is merely indicative.) "Image 1451 shows . . . " counsel intoned, and she was about to explain what it showed and why it had been tabled when one of the sides (the side that had tabled the image) objected. The amount of sun coming through the skylights was not sufficient to view the image properly, this side contended. (I forget which side it was; it doesn't matter.) They asked that the blinds be opened slightly, and that happened. But that, of course, was not the end of the matter.

The other side (the side which had committed the outrage shown in the image) raised a counterobjection: that now there was too *much* light being let in. So, the blinds were adjusted again, and there was less light in the room for a while. Though not for long, because the side which had objected first duly objected for a second time, with the result that the blinds were adjusted for a third time, and more light was thrown on proceedings again. But only for as long as it took the other side to lodge their second objection and insist on a fourth adjustment to the blinds.

And so it went on: ad nauseam if not ad infinitum because, all of a sudden, as often happens, the protagonists tired of the game and an accommodation was quickly reached. Both sides seemed satisfied despite—or perhaps, *because*—the amount of light in the room was—to the neutral eye at least—all but indistinguishable to the status quo ante. At which point I promise to desist from any more schoolboy Latin, but I must quote Behrends's Law, which, if you will recall (*I do recall*), states that: War = the long and bloody route back to square one.

Now, its application to this particular incident is obvious enough, but so too is its application to the wider conflict. For all the indications are that a new peace line will only reinstate the old division of the country; that the post-war settlement will only restore the pre-war balance of power. In other words, if rather inelegantly, all of this just to get back to that.

One last word about the dispute over the blinds. In one sense, nothing was achieved, and we ended up where we started. But in another sense, one side won. A small victory, at least. A temporary advantage. How so?

Simply that, throughout all the back and forth, the image— sometimes in more light, sometimes in less; eventually, in much the same—remained on our screens, and thus imprinted itself on our consciousness in a way that was that bit more compelling than all the other images we viewed that day, thereby putting the side which was alleged to have committed the atrocity shown in the image at a slight disadvantage when it came to us weighing up which of the two sides was the more objectionable. And that no doubt was the reason—or at least, part of the reason—why the issue of the light was raised by the side that did so. For a short while, they had "got one over" on their opponents. They would, they felt, be viewed in a somewhat more favourable light, if you will. And that was important to them, for all that this advantage was short-lived, because they would soon stand accused—with supposed filmed evidence to back it up—of dark deeds of their own.

I try to imagine their thought processes.

Ah, a photograph of one of our soldiers, one of their prisoners-of-war, being crucified. Let's raise an objection about the light in the room. Let's ensure that this hideous image lingers on the screen and is seared into your memory. It will delay too the showing of a video of a member of one of our militia dousing a caged woman hostage in petrol and burning her alive. For that will make us *look bad. There's no escaping the fact. Though we will deny all responsibility for the incident. Suggest the image has been photoshopped. Come up with anything we can think of to distract and deflect. But never mind about that just now, look again at this picture on the screen of our soldier—more a boy, really, sixteen or seventeen at most. They are hammering nails into his hands, he will hang on that cross in heaving agony, until he dies from asphyxiation. Or exposure. Look at it! This is what they do to our people, our young people, our women and children. That's why we need more light. No, that is not enough, open the blinds some more, you need to look at the photograph, really* look *at it. Don't listen to them. Don't let them shroud this atrocity in darkness. Don't you see what they are doing? They don't want you to see the full horror. This is what these animals are like . . .*

You see what we have to contend with? To put up with. To endure, to tolerate, to humour, to *indulge*! Is it any wonder that sometimes one wants to rage and howl? To rain down abuse and contempt. To . . .

One doesn't, of course. One keeps one's cool. Though on this occasion something inside me did snap, because it was with what, in the circumstances, amounted to reckless flippancy that I said: "Gentlemen" (they are, to a man, men), "thank you for coming to a compromise on that question. Perhaps we can carry that spirit into the afternoon session?"

And I then called an immediate adjournment for lunch, signing off with a jaunty rat-a-tat-tat of my gavel. Click. I turn my screen off. And remove my headphones. Click. I turn the screen off in my head. And silence the screams. Click. It is the only way. Click. A spot of lunch now. Think only of that. Of the agreeable hubbub that surrounds the buffet, which is always a splendid one. Click. I think I might have the chicken alla Milanese with the spaghetti in tomato sauce. And then the apple strudel. Click. As a rule, I don't drink at lunchtime. Today, though, I might have a glass or two of red. Click. And I will have a strong cup of coffee after that. And a breath of fresh air. Click. We resume in an hour. Tick. Fifteen minutes now. Tock. But in the meantime. Click. Switch off. Like a machine. It is the only way.

But this time there was no resumption.

Drat my reckless flippancy, my jaunty rat-a-tat-tat.

Three days we have been in shuttle mode now, with both sides refusing to meet in plenary, or indeed to leave their respective floors. And not because of an issue of substance, or because of the argument over the blinds (that is now entirely forgotten), but because of another trivial incident, which took place in the corridor straight after I adjourned the session, in which one side took offence at a perceived slight by the other and the other took offence at being so accused. The same old story, in other words. The same old *fucking, FUCKING, FUCKING* . . . story.

Now, calm down.

These things happen. People have been reminding me of that constantly. And I know it to be true. But the point is this: this particular thing wouldn't have happened if I had only stuck to our scheduled timetable. Then, security staff would have been in place in the corridor to stop just such an unmediated coming-together of the two sides, it being recognised that whenever that happens, *this* happens—that is to say, some petty falling-out—*another* petty falling-out, in a long *series* of petty fallings-out—that derails the talks for days.

I confess I took refuge in one too many glasses of Scotch, as the sound of evening prayers drifted down from the respective floors of the two delegations. (I swear they compete to appear the more devout.) "Bloody hypocrites," I cursed under my breath. Then, more vocally—a colleague sitting in a leather chair close to mine peered over his newspaper or *Magic Mountain*—"Bloody fool." It really is the most dispiriting aspect of such negotiations: spending hours, if not days, if not weeks (sometimes it comes to that), not having the talks we are here for, but having talks about getting the talks back on, or even—once things unravel an unstoppable regression can take hold—talks preliminary to talks to get the talks back on.

My fellow walkers the following morning had the sense and decency to offer no words of consolation or optimism—or indeed any words at all. (The fact that I obviously had a blinding hangover was doubtless another factor in their consideration.) I trudged across the snowfield, over the icy bridge, through the stand of pines and up the steep section . . . absorbed in despond. But as I had hoped—there would have been no early surfacing without that hope—the panorama of peaks lifted my spirits. And on the second walk after the breakdown, two days later, I had the moment of inspiration these walks sometimes supply.

Mea culpa (please forgive) is the gist of it. Our strategy since then has been to convince the parties that no blame lies with either or both of them, but *only* with me: for *my* insensitivity, *my* violation of agreed protocol, *my* deviations from diplomatic norms. And while this constant abasement, offered by me and on behalf of me, is wearing to my sense of self-respect, it has succeeded in wearing *them* down—and that, as we know when we sign up for the diplomatic life, is the name of the game.

"Whatever it takes, gentlemen" (we too were, to a man, men then), I recall old Forrester telling us at the staff college. "And that includes wheedling and pleading. Begging the scum of the earth for forgiveness. *Please, Mr. Scum, please come back to the table, Mr. Scum. Thank you, Mr. Scum. You are a gentleman, Mr. Scum.*" Old Forrester was old school. It's not like that at the staff college these days, I can tell you.

Many more women, for a start. (*Though still too few*, I hear you add.)

Yet I can't lose their respect entirely—these Mr. Scums of the moment. As ever, it is a fine balance. When—let's not go there with *if*—the substantive talks resume, I can see myself deploying a few notably hard raps with my gavel so as to restore myself to tinpot dignity, if not real power, in their eyes. But that is in the hoped-for future. In the meantime:

"Ambassador, may I respectfully suggest once again that the point to focus on here is not the actions of the other party, but *my* actions in precipitating all that followed. Both parties fully agree that my actions were clumsy, to say the least, and although mutual recognition of that fact does not clear up all the other matters of dispute, I am hoping that it can serve as a starting point for a resumption . . . "

We shall see.

One good sign: neither side has walked. They could easily have escalated matters, right up to full suspension, and the fact that they neither embarked on this path from the start, nor have driven themselves down it subsequently, suggests that temporarily collapsing the talks was at least partly tactical. (That it was in other part emotional, even hysterical, goes without saying.) And this means that at some point they will calculate—or at least pretend to themselves—that they have achieved the maximum tactical advantage. And as long as this coincides with a subsidence in emotion (and, more intricately—there are a lot of moving pieces here—with a sense on both sides that the *other* side, but not their own, has been forced to climb down), the full talks will be back on.

"Your optimism is ingenious, Mr. Behrends," the Russian observer said when I gave my report to him. I only just stopped myself from correcting him. "You mean . . . " He didn't, of course. He is much too self-possessed to be *infected* by anything. Ingenuity, on the other hand, is a quality he admires in others as well as himself.

"We're still behind you, all the way," the American observer said with his usual threat-level enthusiasm. "White House, State Department, Pentagon."

"The PM is of course concerned to hear about this latest breakdown," the UK observer observed coolly. "But she has the greatest faith in you, Edvard, you know that."

"What is the English expression? 'A bump on the road'— that's it," the French observer said with a smirk. (I think he puts on the accent. The *French* accent.)

I "retain the confidence" of the Quartet, then. How much confidence I have in myself is another matter.

At present, we are on an adjournment from the adjournment, negotiations to reconvene after the latter, having themselves broken down again. The two parties are locked away on their floors talking only to each other—which is to say, to others in their own party.

Or perhaps they are not even doing that. Perhaps, like me— I have stood down my negotiating team and all the support staff—they are in their own rooms, lying on their beds, missing their homes, their loved ones. Such reflection might just make them think of the benefits of peace, it occurs to me: no more bombing of their homes, no more killing of their loved ones. Or—my thoughts circle back on each other like this all the time—it could as easily drive them to think of leaving the talks, reminding them of why they hate each other so and why making peace would be a betrayal.

Such is the damnable contrariety of this business; this *peace* business.

I am lying on my bed no longer: I have given vertical vent to my frustration by leaping up, striding across the room and pulling open the sliding door to the balcony—the last, a horizontal action, but a great, heaving, heavy one.

That hit. The cold. The clarity. The majesty. The palms of my hands impressed in the stiffening crust of snow on the balcony ledge, I take in, take *on*, the view. That it is mine—*my* view from *my* balcony: a singular configuration of rooftops, snowfields, forest and mountains, twilit by a sky that is a deepening blue and orange bruise—creates a power relationship, a back and forth, almost between *equals*: somehow, all this stupendousness is at my behest. It is all there, laid out before me, as it were, to draw what strength I will from it.

I stand like this sometimes, on the porch of the cabin, in this sort of light or in early light, it doesn't really matter. A drink in hand helps—whisky or a mug of tea with a nip of whisky in it. Clumpy grass, chomped over by clumps of sheep; old Gulbrandsen's raddled woolly bundles. There is invariably one ewe on a rock promontory, chewing gum, ill-fitting dentures, jaws sliding from slide to slide, looking the wrong way, looking at me. It has no appreciation of Caspar David Friedrich or the Lake poets, dumb creature. Blessed creature. We, cursed, cannot look out on all this, there or here, raising our gaze, taking it all in, save through the frame of our making.

Ownership again: the Sublime, capitalised by our contemplation of it.

Up in Urke, the panorama is forbiddingly fjordic of course: slabs of sea mountain, squared-off or brokentoothed, shouldering massively into the Hjørundfjord, or hurtling sheer, hurling cataracts ahead in wild screams of spray. Not that the glacial water of the fjord is much put out. A fair-sized apartment block, human specks crowding the rails, barely murmurs the surface, and by evening—the trolls having tossed away the toy cruise ships—it is glass. Reflecting on infinity.

Indulge me: let me say—with the only twinge of embarrassment coming from that have-it-bothways plea for indulgence—that it puts things into perspective. Little me/all this. The quotidian/deep time. And not one crushing the other, but rather, a throwing-of-an-arm-around, as it were. As if to say: *you are part of all this.* Just a tiny part, mind. Infinitesimally small. But at the same time no belittling. A due relationship is established. Mankind and nature. Mankind and fate. Mankind and—dare I say (you won't like it, but you're not here)—God?

It is why they put us up here, of course. High above the throng. Close to the angels, so to speak. Making of us demiurges. These are immense affairs that we are engaged in. We must pay respect to ourselves for that. (Come out on to your own balconies, I should cry out to every man and woman on the mission, to both delegations. Look out and draw strength, as I am doing.) It is not the petty quibbling of the last few days that defines us, but rather this most noble enterprise: Peacemaking . . .

And yet . . .

In the grand scheme . . .

Night is descending over the now familiar hemicycle of iceblue summits, and one is thankful that here, unlike in Urke, there is the comfort of lights coming on across the darkening valley. All the circuitry of sophisticated civilisation. Liquid light streaming up the sinuous mountain road and disappearing into the underground car parks; lamplight in windows welcoming back parties of skiers to their chalets; hotels and restaurants switching to warm evening après-ski. And fires and lamps are burning rustically in the scattering of farmsteads that still fringe the village, sitting higher on the slopes or deeper down in the valley, where the black river, screened by black pines, seethes under its lid of ice. And all the while, some unseen hand is, one by one, lighting the candles in the churchyard. And then tending the sanctuary lamp in the mountain chapel?

In two banqueting suites in the hotel, cleared out for the purpose, strip lit to their specification, rugs rolled out on the parquet floor, the two warring parties are praying. Facing inflexibly in the same direction. Over the mountains, down to the coast, across the sea, towards the Kaaba. Burning sun and burning sands. Stadium glare illuminating the *sahn*. Hordes of the faithful. Fanatic devotions fuelled by bitter recrimination. Bitter recrimination fuelled by fanatic devotions. Both sides insisting on the indivisible Oneness of Allah.

And trapped inside screens that have been blank for three days the ghost of an image of a young man dying in agony lingers. When we resume, when we turn our screens back on, that image will not be there. Click. A screen saver will appear. A panoramic image, shot from high in the mountains at night, of the resort glittering in the valley. A prospectus for a good life.

Sharp rap of hard wood against sounding block.

W e are resuming in an hour. Who knows how the impasse was broken? One moment, deadlock; the next, a note came down from one floor, quickly followed by a note from the other.

Of course, we are only back where we were four days ago. Indeed, in truth, we have lost ground, as every breakdown drains some of the available energy and goodwill from the substantive proceedings. But think of it this way: it is as if we have been sitting in a traffic jam for ages, and now we are moving again. Whatever the time wasted, however slow the progress ahead, there is release in that sensation of resumed forward motion.

And that's it for this one. I just wanted you to know the good news and to say you shouldn't worry about me. I was feeling pretty low last time. You know how I get sometimes? But I have recovered my spirits.

I will sign off now.

THE HANNAH WÄCHTER MOMENT

There was a time when you liked me to describe in some detail wherever in the world I happened to be at that moment. I want to be able to picture it, you used to say when we spoke on the phone. Why don't you just fly out here? I would reply. And sometimes, in the earlier days, you would. But more often, and more frequently as the years went by, you would laugh at the idea. Not dismissively. The tone was rather: *If only!*

Yet, in truth, the reason you didn't come was not because you couldn't. Or not entirely. Doubtless, some part of you would have liked to be with me, to visit this or that place or another, to have a break from your own frantic work schedule. But in large part you simply had no desire to get away. That frantic work schedule stemmed—branched is a better word: much sturdier—from a job you loved, you lived for. Not quite as much as you loved me or lived for us, perhaps, but not far off.

Don't try to dispute the point. And don't feel bad about it. One thing we never were, was overly sentimental about our relationship. Not at the time anyway—which is the way of it with sentiment, I find. It is more a creature of dewy-eyed contemplation. It is ill-suited to the dry air of the lived present.

And perhaps I am talking more for you than for me, but I nonetheless agree that the facts we "had our own professional and social lives," "didn't live in each other's pockets or under each other's feet," and "both did jobs that meant we spent quite a bit of time apart" were among the reasons we had such a strong bond. These circumstances allowed us to indulge in more sentimentality (which has its place in a relationship) than would otherwise have suited our natures. "Love you," "miss you," "can't wait to see you" are things so much more sincerely said, and truly felt, in the absence of the other, than in their always-somewhat-irksome presence. Which—I know, I know—is pretty much to rewrite, and more ponderously, a greetings-card cliché, but here's the rub: I'm semi-permanently wobbling on the lip of all that is clichéd about bereavement. It is mainly through channelling you that I am able to reflect more rigorously—as I hope I am doing so now—on the condition.

Had we known that one of our lives would be cut short, would we have chosen to spend more time together? Given that every second of the time I spent with you is now so precious to me, it might seem that I would wish it so. But in truth, no. For the preciousness lies partly in the scarcity, but more in the diamond-like precision: the exactitude of the amount of time we had together—both together/together and together/apart (when, after all, we always knew we would be seeing each other again soon). The reality is I cannot have a moment longer with you than I had, or to configure it differently, I don't wish for it. I have made a hard pact with that fact. It preserves me. It honours you. It is true to the spirit of us.

Those days—the describe-in-detail days, that is—came before the era of the Internet, of course; before you could just tap "this place", "that place" or "the other" into a search engine and find its website, its photo gallery, its Wikipedia page; or, via Google maps, float up its streets, inspect every one of its buildings, virtually, and all but zoom in through this window, do an about-turn and look out, as I am doing right now, from this place, Klotild's, a smart café I often visit, just to sit and read and think.

Do I have any friends here? Anyone I can turn to or con-
fide in? These, I fancy, are questions you want to ask of me,
now that there will never again be any flying over, any phone
calls, or Skype calls, or greetings at the airport, or glasses of
wine and swapping of news, standing up at the island in the
kitchen, on that first, that most treasured, evening home. Do
not worry about that, I want to say, lip trembling slightly,
imagining you in a place, a state of being, that seems to me so
crushingly forsaken. Or rather, not imagining you, anywhere
or in any state, except totally lost to me. I have the walking
group, and there are the evenings in the *Gaststube*. I am constantly in the company of colleagues, many of whom I have
known for years.

But is there anyone in particular; a close friend? (You do
not give up. You are determined to make this about me.)

The answer to that is, no. Not here, and sometimes I think,
not anywhere. You are the only close friend I have ever wanted
or needed, which is why being apart from you, and knowing it
is now for ever, is so hard for me.

And that, I realise, sounds heartbreaking, pitiful, though
really, I don't feel sorry for myself so much as for that man,
who happens to be me, who looks so sad and lonely, having a
coffee and a pastry in Klotild's on his own on a bright, crisp
Saturday morning. I'd go as far as to say I feel that catch in the
throat, that lurching feeling, as I contemplate this man's solitude from . . . where exactly? Somewhere in that corner, where
the international newspapers are arrayed on mahogany rods;
just there, where that elegantly jacketed woman is sitting—
though why there, why her, I couldn't say. She doesn't seem in
the least sympathetic—hard-faced would be a better descrip-
tion—and isn't even looking in my direction . . .

Then suddenly she is. And I have to shoot back over here,
to my table next to window, where any sense of myself as a
sorry figure, a man bereft, feels plain daft. Something to do

with perspective, perhaps? I am, if anything, quite content at this moment—which is to say, these little diversions aside, I am a bit lonely, but it is that type of loneliness which reflects rather well on the person so absorbed in it. One can imagine oneself, at this one remove, as the star of an arthouse film or the subject of a classic black-and-white photograph. Cast in this way, framed as if in a lens, sadness and solitude enjoy a 180-degree status change. A certain dignity is conferred. Gravitas. Another word that comes to mind—shades of elegance perhaps—is elegiac. Which is a word that has none of the ugly jagged edges of wretched. Moreover, if I do start to wallow, or indeed indulge myself in any way, I can eventually rely on a practised sense of the absurd to pull me back to the surface. Back to the momentby-moment coordinates we all live by. The constant computing of existence.

Have I lost you with all these convolutions? I wouldn't blame you if I had. I suppose this is what they call a "coping mechanism." And as they also say: it works for me. Whatever it takes. Not Forrester this time, but Caroline, my counsellor. It's not often that she comes to mind. I am pleased to say I have no need of her services now.

I am in decent spirits, then, sitting here in this café, in one corner of the main square in the nearby town, lower in the valley, looking out on the church, with its white tower and green-copper onion dome, to which I will shortly be crossing to attend a chamber-music concert. Haydn quartets.

Then I will have some lunch somewhere and take a short walk around the elegant and expensive shops of this resort. I need—or at least, want—to buy a pair of gloves more suitable for the warming weather. I will return to the hotel for a cup of tea and to read. I may have a short nap. Then I will have an early-evening drink. There will be somebody I can drink with—if I feel the need of company. Then it will be time for dinner. I have booked a table at the best of the Italian restaurants in the town, and a couple of senior colleagues will be joining me. We will talk talks inevitably, but then the conversation will move on to wider geopolitical matters, and to books, plays, films, philosophical this and that. There might even be some more personal chatter, some asking after loved ones. But we won't even try to get below the surface. As I say, they are colleagues. But even if they were friends . . .

And there you have it: another day done. (I almost said, ticked off. Chalked up is better.) It will have been a good day in the way that unremarkable days, of leisurely pursuits and refined entertainment, generally are, I find. Though of course it will have passed without you—I mean, without half the world. (Hikmet, remember? I have been rereading him here as well. The usual tower of books by my bedside.)

When one does supposedly important work—and I will withdraw the unnecessarily defensive "supposedly" straight away . . . we are doing important work here: we are working to end a bloody civil war, for goodness' sake—when one does important work, people imagine that a day away from it must feel like an empty day, a wasted day, not appreciating what I would have thought was obvious: that the importance of our work, and of all the important work in the world, lies in the very fact that if we succeed in it, we will all enjoy more days like the one I will enjoy today: inconsequential, unmemorable, a day in which nothing much is achieved, but no harm is done.

First, do no harm. *Primum non nocere.* I have always liked this principle; a foundational principle of your profession. We would have been in the tiny kitchen of our apartment in Kungsholmen. Those early Stockholm years, so precious to us: the green dotted seascape of the archipelago; the compact cupolaed and spired mass of Gamla Stan. Our first flat, our first home together. My first love. (I forgive you Charlie!) First and last. There will never be another. (Cue violins.) You were always more ambitious for me than I was for myself. (To a large extent, that is true the other way around. Perhaps there is no surer sign of love?) I remember you qualifying, your first registrar's job, your first consultant's position. It really was no great sacrifice on my part to turn down certain postings because they didn't fit around your career. I have never really wanted to be leading the delegation, chairing the talks, sitting at the top table. Such preferment came my way, I'm sure, because I didn't chase it.

I won't pretend it hasn't saved me, though. I would have surely drowned without it. (Cue the whole string section: great soaring, surging strings. Not Haydn.) But if the circumstances had been different I would happily have spent my days on my own, at a table in a café, with a book, achieving nothing much, but harming no one, not just occasionally, but every day, knowing that when I got home, you would be there, at the end of your long, busy, important working day—saving lives.

I must pay. I must get to the concert. Haydn. Quartets 1 and 2, Opus 76. If I was telling a story with a discernible shape, with a narrative arc, I would reveal at this point that these quartets were great favourites of ours, that we had an old vinyl record which we found on a market stall and played over and over while making love on sunny afternoons when we were students. You see how effortlessly the scene is evoked? As it is, I don't remember ever having heard these quartets. Haydn, I know, was no great favourite of yours. And if we ever made love on sunny afternoons . . . I'm joking; *of course* we did . . . it was more likely that Miles Davis was on the stereo. (No strings.)

The word that comes to mind to describe the quartets—I am having lunch at a little place near the ice rink which serves an excellent Tiroler Gröstl (a favourite here)—is divertissement. The second quartet, the programme notes tell me, is known as the "Fifths," after the falling perfect fifths with which it opens. I know I will remember that and will find some opportunity soon to say, "Ah, the Fifths" in a way that will please me no end, despite—no, let me be honest, *because*—I will be picturing you rolling your eyes as I do so.

But there is something I must tell you. I have mentioned before that there is this fellow in one of the delegations who is reading *The Magic Mountain*—in Arabic, though I have no doubt he could manage it perfectly well in English, perhaps even in German. His name is Noor, Dr. Osman Noor, and although he is nominally the number three in his delegation, he has long seemed to us more important than this status would suggest. It could be that this is just our bias towards the more Westernised of the delegates. It is easy to slip into the assumption that they are the ones who—to use Maggie Thatcher's phrase about President Gorbachev—we can more readily "do business with"; that they are more reasonable, more civilised, more decent, more "like us."

My own number three, Cruickshank, has his own way of alerting me when he thinks I am tending too far in this direction. "Orientalism," he mutters under his breath, a reminder of the Edward Said book I gave everyone to read before the talks started; a book you urged on me years ago, and which, as Cruickshank's signalling makes clear, I haven't internalised quite as much as I would like to think.

But to get to the point: Noor was there, at the church. Not at the Haydn quartets, though now I come to think of it, the idea is not so outlandish. Think SS officers attending chamber concerts, within the precincts of Auschwitz-Birkenau, as the gas ovens did their infernal work. "Yes, indeed, Mr. Behrends," I can hear Noor saying, "let us not forget the depths of barbarity into which *this* continent plunged not so long ago." He is adept at turning things back against us in such ways, which given Europe's history is fair enough, I suppose, though he never troubles to distinguish between the various European countries, some of which have been more the victims of barbarity than the perpetrators of it. On top of which, I do take issue with the notion that *all* the world's ills are the fault of the West. Colonisation/decolonisation, intervention/non-intervention, arms sales/arms embargoes, trade/sanctions: we are damned if we do/damned if we don't. And yes, yes, I know . . . Orientalism.

"Mr. Behrends."

"Dr. Noor."

In fact, it was in the churchyard that we bumped into each other. As in the village, every grave in this churchyard is adorned with an elaborately wrought metal cross—all floral motifs and curlicues—rising from a simple marble base. A brass plaque on the shaft of the cross records details of the deceased (often—touchingly—a married couple) and features small oval-shaped portrait photographs, generally showing husband and wife in traditional Tyrolean costume. Black carriage lamps containing red candles are attached to the base of the shaft and there are other candle holders at the foot of the grave. In the evening, all the candles are lit and create a twinkling, festive scene in the snow-quilted churchyard. In the bright sunshine of midday, the aspect is still picturesque, but the ironwork of death stands out in somewhat starker relief.

Having greeted me without any obvious sign of unease, Noor proceeded to anticipate my questions—speaking to me more personally than he had ever done previously, though with his usual clipped formality.

"You are surprised to see me in this place. You would have assumed our religion forbids it. In fact, Islamic teaching is not definitive as to whether visiting the graveyards of Christians is, as we say, *haram.* Some teachers suggest that it is only permissible if you pass on the tidings of hell at the graveside. I can see you find that notion as distasteful as I do. When I was in Paris as a student, many years ago, at a time when, I must admit, I was considerably less devout than I am today, I took to visiting the cemeteries there, and I have continued the practice wherever I happen to be in the world. If nothing else, it is useful to be reminded that most men pass through this life and into the next world without much disturbance to their fellow men, leaving only a small mark—a destiny I sometimes envy."

And with that he gestured with his leather-gloved hand towards the grave beside him, only to find when he looked down at the inscription that it read: *Hannah Wächter, b.1928 d.2000.*

It was, for a moment, an awkward moment, but then Noor saved himself—and me—by laughing. Quite a guffaw, in fact. Most surprising coming from a man of such steely self-control.

"My apologies to you, Fräulein Wächter," he continued, still with a twinkle in his eye. "I know nothing of you except what is recorded here. But it alone is evidence of a life well spent."

Eine liebende Schwester und Tante.

We stood in silent contemplation for a moment or two and then I said: "I will leave you in peace."

I meant nothing in particular by it; it was simply the pleasantry that came to mind. Noor replied with some force, however. Not angrily, but with palpable emotion. He apparently took my words to have a wider application. "You must realise, Mr. Behrends, that we all fervently wish for that end."

My initial reaction—it will not surprise you—was caution. I didn't say anything; I simply nodded my head. I had heard him, I indicated, but I didn't have a view. Noor directed his attention at me. It should have been the time for me to look away. But for some reason I didn't. Indeed, I held his gaze. More than that, my eyes were positively eloquent. I didn't have a view, they explained, because I *couldn't* have a view. He must understand that, they insisted. Consider my position, they added—the jarring note. The connection was lost. It was Noor who looked away.

I was disappointed. Damn my caution, I thought, just for a moment. Though a moment later I was thinking, no, I am right to be cautious, it is my job, my *duty*, to be cautious. I was thinking, rather belatedly, about how our encounter might look: the two of us having a private—one might almost say, surreptitious—conversation in a quiet churchyard, not just outside the complex, but away from the resort. In our line of work people have a tendency, and rightly so, to view such encounters with suspicion. And while for me that could be professionally damaging, for Noor it could be personally dangerous.

Yet that led me to this reflection: that I didn't doubt for a moment Noor's sincerity, or that he had spoken spontaneously. I even felt that he had meant, and wanted me to know it, that the "all" included the other delegation. In other words, there was no stratagem here. No playing for advantage. He hadn't been put up to it. He had spoken from the heart. He had simply said what he wanted to say, *needed* to say perhaps. Not so much to me, as to himself.

You must remember that a negotiator at peace talks has always the mindset of a warrior. For all that the theatre of war has shifted, he is no less on the battlefield. War is his imminent default; peace only a distant prospect. If he thinks otherwise, he might as well surrender; have peace at any price. And what man stoops to that abjection? Yet peace is the prize to be seized in this theatre. And on the right terms, it is a victory of sorts. At least, it is to the type of warrior I now took Noor to be: the type that wants to win, but not to destroy, to annihilate. The man who would win the peace, amass its spoils, claim and proclaim that glory, rather than apportion obliteration. We look for these types during negotiations; they are key to any chance of success. So, perhaps, after all, there was some signalling in Noor's words. *You can work with me.* Which might have been a heartfelt human plea or something more tactical. Or a bit of both.

As you can see, my thoughts were paddling frantically. Perhaps I am reading too much into a single remark? But remember it came after Noor talking about his faith and the shared Hannah Wächter moment. The fact is the encounter with Noor put me in good spirits: the theme of the day. I tucked into that Tiroler Gröstl at lunchtime and did all the other things I mentioned with a lighter heart than of late, with a new spring in my step.

A mong my night-time reading these last couple of months (and indeed for quite some months before I came out here) has been Rebecca West's monumental *Black Lamb and Grey Falcon*. (Quite impossible at the breakfast table, I find.) I am nearing the end now—less than 50 of the 1,150 pages to go.

What is it about a really big book? (Don't answer.) I am drawn to them anyway. Remember my Proust years? A good three, as I recall, with time off for thrillers, for Wodehouse, and for the slightly less heavy ordinance from the canon. Imagine: Dostoyevsky by way of light relief! It came to that.

But let me read this section to you.

Human beings are not reasonable, and do not in decisive degree prefer the agreeable to the disagreeable. Only part of us is sane: only part of us loves pleasure and the longer day of happiness, wants to live to our nineties and die in peace, in a house that we built, that shall shelter those who come after us. The other half of us is nearly mad. It prefers the disagreeable to the agreeable, loves pain and its darker night despair, and wants to die in a catastrophe that will set back life to its beginnings and leave nothing of our house save its blackened foundations. Our bright natures fight in us with this yeasty darkness, and neither part is commonly quite victorious, for we are divided against ourselves and will not let either part be destroyed. This fight can be observed constantly in our personal lives. There is nothing rarer than man who can be trusted never to throw away happiness, however eagerly he sometimes grasps it. In history, we are as frequently interested in our doom. Sometimes we search for peace, sometimes we make an effort to find convenient frontiers and a proper fulfilment for racial destinies; but sometimes we insist on war, we stamp into dust the only foundations on which we can support our national lives.

First, I know that you would rather I didn't read out such long passages. *I have my own book to read, Ed.* But you must admit that is good. *Yeasty* darkness. What does that mean in this context? Turbulent or something? It doesn't matter, though, does it? It *feels* just right. But why did I want to read out this passage, late at night, just before going to sleep? Wasn't the theme of the day good spirits? So why such relish for something so dark, so bleak?

I can't really explain, except to say (not for the first time): human nature. We are contrary buggers. Divertissement has its place. I might read a few pages of Wodehouse right now. But when I finally turn the bedside light off, I will turn the radio *on*, and I will fall asleep—I swear I am *lulled* by it—to the BBC World Service news.

More than a hundred confirmed dead in a car-bomb explosion in Lahore . . .

S leep in general, though, remains a slippery customer. Observably—if my sleep was being monitored by researchers, or you were watching over me all night—I am, no doubt, much more asleep than awake. Yet my perception—which is all, in the end, that counts for me—is that I am, if not constantly awake, then constantly *waking*, which is hardly restful, involving as it does a constant cycle of upheavals—from unconsciousness to consciousness and back again; from the dream world to the real world to the dream world—pinging back and forth between one crazy universe and another, the waking state being the less crazy of the two, but perhaps only because it gets to pathologise its rival.

And yes, having woken, I do tend to drop back to sleep "just like that," as you—never a great sleeper yourself and so well-placed, you liked to claim, to assess my sleep patterns—would say. But if this is true—and I will admit I never have any memory of this dropping back to sleep being much of an effort—that doesn't mean I am sleeping soundly. I am getting quite a lot of sleep across the night, perhaps, but in short bursts: stop/start, stop/start, stop/start. Toss/ turn, toss/turn, toss/turn.

You get some sense of how irritating it must be? Stop/start/toss/turn. *Yes, I get it.* And then there is this unnerving nerve-tingling in my feet: a fizziness, as if my feet are feeling anxious, getting restless, want to know where they stand. And this sensation rises up through the rest of me, so that in the end *I*—the conscious entity—am the one that is anxious, restless, fizzing, sensational, kicking off the bed covers, having yet another sip of water, turning on the bedside lamp, reading for a bit, turning off the bedside lamp, tuning in—for solace—to a delirium of atrocity: *This is BBC News* . . .

Of course, I sleep a lot better now than I did, in the days, weeks, after. Back then—and how much longer than two years ago it seems—I was excoriated by the double demand of grief: pain and guilt; agony and inadequacy; that for all my suffering I was not suffering enough. At night this meant that while I observed the ritual of going to bed, *lying* in bed, whenever I was swayed by sleep, lulled towards it, I pulled myself up violently. There was something in this of the man lost in the snow, freezing cold, so tempted to let go, but forcing himself to maintain consciousness. *I must stay awake, I must stay awake.* Did I imagine that if I could only keep my eyes open, fight sleep off, *you* would somehow defeat death? That slumped unslumbering over your sheeted body in this mausoleum of the imagination I would feel you stir? That those stony lips would twitch and pout—and breathe? Perhaps. At my most crazed—crazed with grief, crazed with exhaustion. Those nights appear as daguerreotypes. Mercury vapour on silver screen. A swirl of ghosts in the monochrome.

There was self-indulgence in this sleepless vigil, I'll admit. Or at least a large element of self-protection—as there is in every sought martyrdom. Jagging grief, hurling oneself on to the rocks, then hauling oneself out on the rip, again and again and again, was slowly numbed into an exercise in sheer endurance. The pain moved out of body, hovered just above me, and while it was no less intense, it was increasingly ecstatic. I was moving towards something. Light at the end of the tunnel, if you will.

After a few nights I abandoned our bed for the double in the spare room, then the other guest bed in my study, and then the put-you-up in yours. On or rather *from* that—by far the most uncomfortable of the beds by any normal standards—I drew some comfort, some peace. More likely, of course, it was from being in that room. That room of yours, with its quiddity of you. The vestigial thingness of you. Just normal stuff: books, paintings, CDs, knick-knacks, I suppose you would call them. Nothing very special, but through abrupt abandonment suffused with significance. They, the things, seemed bewildered, heartbroken, by your absence. They seemed lost, not knowing where to put themselves. I moved them around a lot, I will admit. Obsessively, perhaps. (I have them, and hold them, still. Some of them.)

Let's not even start on my sliding into your wardrobe, sliding the doors closed and losing myself among silks and swirls, still smelling of you . . . Your clothes I was eventually persuaded to part with. Car shipments of grief off to the charity shops. That clearout did me good. It hollowed me out.

But I am getting ahead of myself.

On the put-you-up I slept wretchedly, even if you will not allow—even during the worst of it—that I didn't sleep at all. Why, when you were irretrievable, were you still so immanent? I wondered. You were just there, I could swear, just below the surface—and yet out of reach. Trapped, smiling up, beneath a lid of ice. I SMASHED through it, but you had dived. Quicksilver in the black. Or I dashed my fists to stumps on that glass. Your face fading in the blood mist. Why didn't you come when I called, when I cried and cried and cried? Couldn't you hear me? How could you have left me in this state? This, this, this . . . It was this—I give in; you win—which wore me down eventually. Sleep, catatonic almost, claimed me. What a plethora of postures I must have adopted in those shattered intervals? Their monstrosity would have been wondrous to observe given the twisted shapes I found myself in on waking: head and arms hanging rag doll over the side of the bed; a smashed body at all angles on the pavement after a fall from a high building; a spastic child in a flop state. Were you watching over me, rearranging me, your plaything—a ghost toying? The days? I had energy enough only to describe myself as— give me strength—*sleepwalking* through them. I was no better than a zombie, the living dead. I tried to work; I *went* into work. What was I thinking? Doing? Everything took place miles away, behind a smeared screen, through thick foam. I was wading through glue.

Some muscle memory was at work, if you'll forgive two misconceptions—that the brain is a muscle and that muscle memory exists. You won't? *Huh!* I did stuff anyway. Work and the like. It was remarked on as remarkable. I was much praised for my courage. Call it autopilot then, I am too tired to care any more. At meetings, even when I was chairing, I rocked, I lolled, my head describing circles, circles . . . until my crashing chin was caught by an upper cut, out of thin air, knocking my head back and bringing me to. Where were we? Giddy rounds of it.

Then one day, after hauling myself home, much as men might haul a boat up a beach, I fell asleep sitting upright at the kitchen table. Transferred to bed I know not how—something, some*one* must have carried me there—I slept for a week, a month, a second, a night. How long doesn't matter, only how *deep!* Oceanic oblivion. Unfathomable. Nothing then or now has surfaced from that sleep. What went on down there, stays down there. Then, suddenly, I exploded back into consciousness. It was the bends. The most excruciating headache, and violent nausea, and then total exhaustion. I had—hear this—to take to my bed! And then for days afterwards I was as fragile as glass, a crystal bell ringing out my recuperation.

I had experienced, and recovered from, some sort of physical and emotional crash, certainly. But would I describe it as catharsis? Would that it was ever that neat: life, that is, lived in the direction of travel. Looking back, it marked the end of the first phase, I'll go as far as to say that. Something had been processed, worked through, just as a foreign body works its way through the system, is expelled by the violent actions of fever and delirium. I was now teary, sorry for myself, sentimental, occasionally hysterical, bad-tempered towards everyone, constantly weary, drinking too much, eating too little, then too much, but I was functioning after a fashion.

And—yes, I must concede—*sleeping.*

Stop/start, stop/start, stop/start.

Toss/turn, toss/turn, toss/turn.

DAYS

I have nothing to tell you. By which I mean I could tell you in detail about our progress on this or that issue, or indeed our setbacks on others, but it would be a grind for you, as it was for us. And I could tell you about walks and dinners and conversations and books, but I would find myself repeating myself.

Peace talks settle into this repeating pattern after a while, a pattern like that of the floor carpets in places like this conference centre, in which a polygonal weave mesmerises the eye almost to a vanishing point. There is a door at the end there somewhere, one of those doors with a bar release mechanism, on which one pushes down with both hands to exit in an emergency, or at some point when to get out of here is simply imperative.

There. One steps out into fresh snow, crisp in the crepuscular cold, and breathes it in in deep draughts—outside air!— even though this is the area where they bring in the deliveries. It is the designated smoking zone for the kitchen staff. Mainly migrant workers. Sending texts to wives and girlfriends back home. In Innsbruck or Izmir. There is a high security fence; a security light has come on. A few more intakes, and then one must step back in. We will be resuming in five minutes.

One lingers. That hallucinatory air of *The Magic Mountain* again. Time expanding to account for a lack of incident. The narcotic effect of day after day after day. A slow, sweet sinking towards some sort of resolution that might as well be death.

Our guests can leave at any time, descend to their flatlands. This security is for their own protection. The hotel and conference complex has been chosen for its location some way from the resort itself. We are somewhat cut off. But our guests are free to come and go. We all are.

But something, above all the hypnotic rhythm of the days, makes us stay. Another day, another day.

A Book

T hat, I thought, is either a book or a bomb.
It was quite some conclusion to jump to, I acknowledge—particularly as actual jumping (backwards) took
place. For to be more precise, I jumped straight to the "or" not
the "either," the "either" not being a jumping matter for me,
even jumping for joy, pleased as I always am—don't get me
wrong—to receive a book.

Indeed, a book only really entered the equation—at this
point in my thought processes at least—in the sense that I
thought: that is a bomb *designed* to look like a book, or rather
a package designed to look like it contains a book when in fact
it contains a bomb. For this is how they would think, I
thought, perhaps not thinking entirely straight. They would
think: don't make the bomb too obviously bomb-*like*. Don't
make it black and spherical, for instance, the colour and size,
more or less, of a bowling "wood," but with a pipe-cleaner
thing sticking out of the top, fizzing like a sparkler. And don't
even consider the bundle of red sticks of dynamite, with an
old-fashioned alarm clock strapped to it, one of those ones
with two silver bells on the side of its head, that at any moment
the hammer device will start clattering, setting off the detona-
tor and then . . . BOOM!

This was a serious incident, after all, not a Tom and Jerry
cartoon. These are sophisticated terrorists we are talking about
not, not . . . Tom and Jerry.

At which point I thought: security. Where were they? Those

guards in black uniforms with the word "Security" stitched in white and red on their breast pockets. Why hadn't they cleared the corridor, evacuated everyone from the building? Why hadn't I, in my striped pyjamas, via my balcony, via the elevated platform of the local fire and rescue vehicle (though I also had uncomfortable visions of a canvas-seat and rope-pulley contraption), been transported out of harm's way? Where was that robot resembling a vacuum cleaner purring down the carpet to check out this book-like package that any fool could see was actually a *bomb*? Where was the sniffer dog? Where was the bomb disposal team, for fuck's sake?

And just think, I thought, all this is happening on my birthday, a day on which, yes, it might be argued, the chances of someone leaving a book outside my room were that much increased, whereas the chances of someone leaving a bomb were . . . much the same as any other day. That is to say, vanishingly small, negligible to the point of non-existent, but don't forget that there at my feet was this book-shaped package. And these are just the dastardly games these cunning devils play, are they not? The birthday boy, thinking your way, tears open the yellow quilted envelope, a Jiffy bag, disgorging that strangely disagreeable grey fluff, which isn't, but reminds one of, asbestos, expecting to find a book, only to . . .

It hardly spoils the story now . . .

Find a book.

Don't laugh at me.

Sorry.

You should be.

I am, Ed. Too late now.

You were always so dismissive of the possibility that anything like this could happen to you. *What are the odds, Ed?* And you would go on about being struck by a meteorite or winning the lottery or a millionto-one other things that were never going to happen. And you convinced me, Anna. You had me there. You had me thinking it was foolish to worry when in fact I was right to. For it turned out that you were tempting fate, daring the gods to prove you wrong. A dangerous game, gods or no gods. Because—get this—*someone* has to be: the one, that is. That's how the odds work, Anna. At a million to one someone is the one. And it had to be you.

So, yes, *that* might have had something to do with it: that if a meteorite can strike once, then why not twice? That losing you isn't going to spare me. And don't forget either *the car-bomb explosion in Lahore*. My constant diet. But more than that—more to the *point*, I can hear you saying (you weren't going to have me pin this all on you for long)—we are on the highest state of alert here; the security people—they do exist—are constantly urging us to be vigilant. For we all know that there are various factions who want to see these peace talks break up and who would have no hesitation in resorting to terrorism to bring about that end. I might not be the first target for such an attack; the negotiators from the warring parties, and in particular their leaders, are those most under threat, both from extremists on their own side, as well as diehards among their opponents. But as chair of the talks I have had my own briefings on things to look out for, one of them being, yes, Jiffy bags, which have been sent to people in my sort of position at various times and have been found to contain not explosives in fact, but dangerous chemicals, capable of causing nasty burns, or in other incidences, hazardous powders, including anthrax, which can of course prove fatal.

The fact is, I should have called security. Followed procedures. But having been so convinced it was a bomb one moment, I was just as convinced that it wasn't the next. Hence my picking up the package, tearing it open, finding it was . . .

Yes, yes, got that. Is there any more to this tale?

Suddenly you are sounding irritable. Impatient with me. Dare I say, more like your old self!

Yes, I remembered it is your birthday. Yes, I shouldn't have dismissed your concerns like that. Yes, I miss you. Yes, I love you. But at some point . . .

Here's the thing, then: it wasn't just any old book. It was, some might say, *the* book. To those of a certain persuasion at least. *The Noble Quran*, as the title on the cover described it.

I wasn't, as it happened, that surprised. Indeed, at the risk of going all mystical—*please don't*—once I had decided the package did contain a book, the book I thought it would most likely be was the Koran (to revert to the English rendering I am more familiar with, more comfortable with indeed, strange as that might sound). And that was because by then I was certain who the book was *from*—a little card dropped out right on cue: Noor.

A small matter first: it wasn't a birthday card, and the book wasn't a birthday present. But please don't think I am feeling sorry for myself. True, there were no other cards or presents left with my bundle of newspapers on this my birthday. But the occasion wasn't forgotten by my colleagues, who all signed a joint card which they presented to me at teatime, when there was also a small cake with a candle and a mumbled rendition of "Happy Birthday."

Of course, the two delegations did not join in. We do not fraternise in this way. And I have no reason to suppose Noor even knew it was my birthday. The little card certainly did not suggest so. The message inside read simply:

Dear Mr. Behrends
In hope of peace
Best wishes
Dr. Noor

Yet, simple as it was, innocent as it might seem, the message, the gift, above all the sender, begged a lot of questions, all of which started hurtling around inside my head, believe me. A flavour of my initial reaction can be gauged by my physical responses.

First—to go over some of the same ground again—there was the opening of my door; then, the jumping back in shock at seeing the package. This was followed by a sort of tiptoeing back towards the package as I weighed up the bomb/book options in the way I have described at length already. Next, we have the tearing open of the package, with rather a reckless flourish, I might add. Then the book, the note. And to get to the point: what followed was a furtive look, left and right, to see if anyone had witnessed all or any of this, and even a glance up to see if there was CCTV in the corridor. (There wasn't, which is perhaps a security lapse, but not one at that moment I was greatly concerned about.) Finally, there was the dive back into my suite, which, in line with the cartoonish nature of the episode, had something of the quality of the last of the bath-water disappearing down the plughole, or of a tiny object being sucked up by a vacuum cleaner. Left, right, back, slam: I was inside my room again. No one had seen a thing. Phew.

As I say, cartoonish.

Yet as I sat on my bed, with my copy of the noble book on my lap, I felt a sense of profound serenity settle over me. I was centred, still, in the moment and beyond it. Was this the place that Caroline said I would reach if I followed the techniques that she had taught me? Had I suspended my scepticism about letting myself just be? Maybe, though by asking myself the questions I was already lapsing out of it. Still, I didn't fall prey to "What is he up to? What is his game?" type thoughts. Indeed, I was struck by how tiresome it is to think like this: taking nothing at face value, sifting everything through a fine mesh of suspicion, attributing a base—or at least, an ulterior—motive to all actions. Yes, I am the chair of these peace talks, I said to myself, but I am also a human being, and a fellow human being has reached out to me, first in the churchyard, now by giving me a copy of this book, so precious to him, out of respect, kindness—dare I say it—*friendship*, so the least I can do is receive it in that spirit. I was so cheered by these thoughts that for a moment I was almost euphoric. Life is good; the world is good; *men* are good, I found myself thinking. It is not incantation I am generally given to. In my line of work, little evidence is advanced to support it.

And, as I say, the feeling didn't last. That it didn't doesn't matter. Just as it doesn't matter that I won't do more than flick through the pages of the Koran. It is not aimed at me, is all I can say, having tried and failed to make any headway with it on a number of previous occasions. What matters is the gesture, the hope, even expectation, that I would appreciate this gift, for the circumstances in which it was given, but more than that, because of who had given it. And if that makes me an old softy, perhaps even a *dangerous* old softy, so be it.

Noor, of course, gave nothing away all day—in any sense. There wasn't a glimmer, a flicker. The opposite, in fact. Doubtless, he went extra hard just so I didn't get the wrong idea—an approach I must say I respected. We broke up early. "Gentlemen, I don't think there's much prospect of progress in the remaining hour we have scheduled, and it has been a day of intense negotiation, so can I suggest an early adjournment? Please wait in the auditorium until we get clearance to leave." I had half an eye on my birthday tea, I will admit. (I had an inkling the team were planning something.) After it, a smaller number joined me in the bar. Then I had dinner with my deputy, Valery. A working dinner.

It wasn't a late night; we have a long day tomorrow. I put the birthday card on my desk in my suite, next to the never-to-be-opened-again Koran. I had a text message from your brother. It was decent of him to remember, I thought. He never used to before.

De Vries in den Herren

T he rich colour must have come from the red wine sauce, the density from the bread dumplings, texture from the cranberries and red cabbage, and the stinging heat from the Hungarian paprika. That at least was my first thought; my gut instinct, as it were. But then I calculated that the wild boar goulash, last night's main course, could not possibly have worked its way through me so quickly. Despite appearances, what I was confronted with was in fact more likely composed of the previous night's pike and boiled potatoes, yesterday morning's Bircher muesli and pastries, and the cold cuts, potato salad, sauerkraut and pickles from the lunchtime buffet—and indeed meals from earlier in the week.

All those who are not German or Austrian among us—and even the younger ones of them—affect to be appalled by the traditional arrangement at the *Herren* in the *Gaststube*, whereby the sitter, on rising, is invited to study the result of his exertions, laid out laboratorially, so to speak, on a pristine porcelain shelf. I suspect, however, that I am not alone in allowing myself a moment or two of fascinated inspection. And a moment or two more to relish the stench which, such is its powerful intimacy, calls to mind Dr. Freud's deranging scatomancies—"look at me, play with me, love me . . . "

(I can see the look on your face, by the way. How I *love* that look. How I love the cry of *Ed!* You scrunch your nose, shiver in disgust, act as if you are appalled, but you know very well that a love story truthfully told would be as full of shared poos and farts and bottoms and willies, as it would indeed of *fuck me harders* and *suck my dicks* and *eat my pussys*. And don't *Ed!* me about those either because I *know* they really turn you on. *Make me wet, oh Jesus, I'm coming, coming . . .* One might almost say true love only exists when two people share without inhibition such baby talk, such dirty talk; when there are no limits to filthy intimacy.)

But enough of this. There! The dry suction on the flush of these toilets is such that even the heaviest of deposits whooshes down and around the bend like a Bond villain imploding out through a broken plane window. All that remains on the shelf is a smear, a smear which annoyingly is never quite cleared by the whirlpool of water that follows. Some scrupulous brush-work with what the Germans call—delightfully, I think—the *Klobürste* is always required.

I make this observation, I realise, as if toilet-bowl cleaning is common practice among men, whereas in fact there are many who are happy (the word is well chosen) to leave more than a smattering (likewise) of faecal evidence behind. Some remnant of territorial marking? They are contemptuous of the *Klobürste*, or the squirt of toilet cleanser or air freshener, or a slight plumping of the potpourri, or a wiggling of the reed diffusers in the very smartest establishments, which this, of course, is. Your brother springs to mind. Not *Ed!* this time but *Max!*

However, it was not a man of your brother's type who emerged from a cubicle near the far wall just as I was emerging from the cubicle nearest the exit. That was evident from the look of wild panic in his eyes when he saw me. In-and-out-with-out-beingseen-leaving-behind-as-little-evidence-of-occupancy-as-possible: this would have been his strategy, as it was mine.

On finding any of the stalls occupied when we entered the Gents, or indeed on hearing other men take up positions while we were in position ourselves, our intention is to outsit these other occupants, however long it takes. Business has still to be done, of course, but our tactic in these circumstances is to sync our exertions with the sonic cover provided by the unabashed actions of these other occupants. And only when we have heard the dry gulp of the flush, the unlocking of the cubicle door, the torrent from the taps and the blast of the hand dryer (once, twice or however many times), do we dare to venture out.

But there is an occupational hazard for our type of man: namely, that we cannot account for others of our type, other surreptitious shitters, as it were, who, hearing no sound where moments before there had been the elephants playing tubas, barrel bombs dropped at low altitude into deep water, and all the rest of it, assume the coast is clear, only to find ourselves approaching the wash basins side by side, faced with just the prospect we had hoped to avoid, its most dreaded element being the requirement to acknowledge each other in some way, to share a pleasantry or two.

By contrast, your brother's type of man is not only untroubled by such a scenario, he positively relishes it. "My word, that's a load off my mind" or "Good luck to the next man who goes in there." Or, more directly, "Nothing like a good shit, is there?" All things I, and maybe this man next to me, might say to you, his wife, in our respective boudoirs of filthy intimacy, but which we wouldn't dream of saying to another man, in this case, each other, even though—had the situation been only slightly reconfigured—we would have been comfortable enough, flies open, cocks in hand, standing shoulder to shoulder, aiming a steady stream, and perhaps even a thunderous one, into the teardrop urinals. And I have been saying "this man" as if I didn't know who it was, whereas in fact I did, of course. We are a relatively small team.

De Vries, his name is. A Dutchman. A serious fellow, notably conscientious about his work, even among a notably conscientious team. *My* team, I thought with fierce affection, despite the excruciating situation. Silky blond hair, feminine almost, though thinning on top, De Vries wears those now rather old-fashioned-looking wire-framed spectacles, which always seem to have the effect of making the eyes of the wearer look tired, rubbed raw, red-rimmed. On the one previous occasion when we had shared a few words unrelated to the talks, he had pointed me in the direction of an almond slice on the teatime buffet table which he said was particularly delicious. We had enjoyed a good session that afternoon; spirits were high. A shard of flaky pastry had adhered to his upper lip, I noted. I might have pointed it out to him, but didn't, and it remained there—a hanging shard, I thought to myself, apropos of nothing in particular—for several minutes of the after-tea proceedings until, prompted by some sensation, he obliterated it with a moist-tongued cow lick.

Back at the basins it was De Vries who broke the silence. "I have been meaning to say for some time," he began, apparently casually, though I knew what effort it was costing him to say anything to me in these circumstances. Rather to my surprise he had begun inspecting himself in the subtly lit and outrageously flattering mirror above the basins. Any man with an eye to his appearance would be pleased at what he sees in this mirror—I always marvel at how handsome and distinguished (and young) I look. But De Vries looked pained. Though not, I fancied, by mere surfaces. Indeed, as he removed his wire-framed spectacles and peered more deeply into the glass, it was as if he was looking into his own soul, the anguish therein, the fathomless agony . . . Though he might just have been examining his blackheads, of course. "That I am very sorry for your loss . . . "

Having allowed myself to be diverted by thoughts of De Vries looking deeply into his soul or examining his blackheads, I was particularly taken aback to hear him say such a thing. *The* thing, no less. Had he been looking in my direction rather than being absorbed in the various etc., etc., etc., he would have registered the consternation on my face and left it there, perhaps. As it was, he ploughed on—regardless, one might say: "I know it was a couple of years ago now . . . " He had finished with the mirror and was washing his hands thoroughly, fussily, downright annoyingly, under the laser-activated tap " . . . but I imagine the pain doesn't lessen to any great extent." He withdrew his hands suddenly and shook off what water remained. "The thought of being without my Suzy, of losing my Suzy like that . . . "

He trailed off and I, still shocked, still at a loss as to how to react, was struck first by the fact that his wife was called Suzy—pronounced *Soo-zee* (oozingly)—a most unlikely, unsuitable, even rather obscene name for the woman in a man like De Vries's life, I felt. I could imagine him with an Angela or a Marion or even a Theresa, but a *Suzy?* Categorically, no.

"Well, it must be terrible," De Vries concluded, and before proceeding to the hand dryer and exiting, never again to share more than a couple of words with me, more than likely, he patted me on the shoulder, in a most bathetic gesture of brotherliness.

I stood over the basin for some time after De Vries's departure. More for something to do than anything else, I splashed water on my face, as if to recover myself. Though I wasn't feeling particularly emotional. God knows, sometimes a wave of grief overwhelms me. I stagger and bow, heart heaving, legs folding. I have to stop what I am doing, excuse myself, take a break . . .

But this time was not like that. It was more that I was appalled by De Vries's . . . I can think of no other word for it . . . *tactics.* He had found himself in an awkward situation, as I have detailed perhaps tiresomely, but, for God's sake, it was only that I knew he had just been having a shit. That's all. The top and bottom of it, if you will. What sort of man decides in such circumstances to—excuse me shouting—EXTEND HIS CONDOLENCES. And well beyond the point at which they can be extended without being, I would suggest, actively inappropriate. A man who doesn't really know me, and certainly didn't know you, and has no reason, no business, feeling sorry for either of us, but who—and this hit me hard—obviously *did* feel sorry. Or at least, he had imagined what it must be like, and felt the pain of it, or the shadow of the pain of it—that cloud which blocks the sun for a moment—and wanted to communicate that. He had read somewhere that one of the most hurtful things for people who are bereaved is that nobody talks to them about the person they have lost, for fear of causing upset, or saying the wrong thing. That old cliché. That patent untruth.

"Fuck you!" I mouthed angrily at the door through which De Vries had passed, out of my life (I could be pretty certain of that after this, after all). "Fuck you and fuck Suzy"—adding, for good measure, the finger, which I had speedily to withdraw, or rather, to convert into some sort of vague, fluttery gesture with my hand—think a magician Abracadabraing—as another man, right on cue, entered the washroom.

"Are you all right, Edvard?" this other man said. (It doesn't matter what he is called. He isn't going to feature again. Though, as his use of my Christian name suggests, he knows me quite well. Much better than De Vries.) I suppose he thought I was in some distress, had been crying even, had for some reason been thinking of you, as if I don't think of you all the time, as if I am not addressing these thoughts, and all my thoughts, to you constantly, incessantly, never letting you rest, sleep, *go* . . .

STOP.

"I am, François, thank you," I replied breezily. (Okay, his

name is François. But you didn't need to know that, or to know any more about him.) "In fact, I have just had . . . "

I paused for effect; I could hardly believe I was going to say this " . . . the most massive dump."

And with that—it was hugely liberating, I have to say—I marched out.

Too Much?

You didn't like that last one very much, I can tell. Perhaps you are right; perhaps it is the sort of tale— for all that it happened to me and could never happen to him—that a man like Max could carry off, but not me.

(I am seeing Max next week, incidentally. In Berlin, for the opening of his new show in the city. Emboldened by the text message he sent to me on my birthday, I invited myself. I will have some meetings while I am there, of course. I was planning to go anyway at some point. A quick circuit of the capitals.)

I wanted to strike a somewhat lighter note, that is all. It is sometimes hard to know how to pitch things, what to include and what to leave out. I don't know what you will be interested to hear these days. What I can say and what I can't. The situation is not dissimilar to the days when we were first going out together, first getting to know each other; when we *didn't* know each other in fact, at least, not very well—and there were misunderstandings and missteps, often quite trivial, but which could have jeopardised everything and ended it all almost before it began. Each going our own separate ways. Never to have lived and loved. One shudders to think how easily, how carelessly.

I watched a television drama recently in which a couple were having an affair. It's called *The Affair* and it has in it that actor who you used to like from *The Wire*. I can't remember who recommended it. After a sex scene, we see the young woman in the bathroom, washing her hands. The man comes in, naked, flips up the toilet seat and starts to pee. "Too soon?" he says, seeing the girl's look of surprise, slight disgust, even alarm.

Sometimes I feel that the ground has shifted back to those early days. I am not sure where I stand. Too soon? Too much?

For one thing, I haven't heard from you in a while.

Nothing in your voice.

Nothing back.

It was getting fainter, more infrequent anyway. Conventional wisdom has it that this is a good sign. But conventional wisdom gets these things all wrong, I've found. I remember Caroline laughing at me saying that.

It is an odd thing about our much-recorded life together that I don't have a recording of your voice. I can hear it in my mind's ear, though. Yes, the music and the modulation of your voice—quite low and husky (we used to laugh about that; the husky way you said "husky"). I can hear it now. But it is as if you have stopped talking to me.

Well, it's not as if that didn't happen sometimes. Still nothing.

GHENT

T he city has a population of more than a quarter of a million people, and it is just half an hour from Brussels, but for many years Ghent was "our secret." For one thing, few of our friends back then, all of whom had been to Bruges and many to Antwerp, had visited Ghent. Some even claimed not to have heard of it. Or only very vaguely. It was, as you once put it—anticipating that things would change—like an "indie band before it charts."

Our lasting attachment to Ghent stemmed, as these attachments often do, from having had an especially lovely time the first time we were there. I can't recall the exact occasion—it wasn't a birthday or anniversary, I know that much—but everything was just right. It was wintertime: cold and blue, cold and black—with stars! Our visit was neither too long, nor too short—a long weekend, probably. The hotel was boutique before that just meant small and overly expensive. We found a little restaurant which we knew on the first night—and declared as much—would become a regular haunt thereafter. And rather surprisingly—you were never much of a lover of medieval art otherwise—Ghent's most famous attraction, *The Adoration of the Mystic Lamb*, made a deep impression on you. We went to see it twice on that first visit and returned on every subsequent trip.

We never tried to analyse our love for Ghent, though such an exercise would have been easy enough. It was eminently suited to our "High European" sensibility; our love of history, of art, of architecture, of culture generally; of good food, good wine, good living. But it was quirky too, a bit boho with it; a student town as well as a tourist town, though this element did little more than add a plastering of posters to café noticeboards or a pile-up of locked bikes to railings or some early-hours hooting and laughter from below our hotel window. We didn't mix with any students—or locals.

Of course, this ridiculous, this delicious, idea that Ghent was somehow "discovered" by us was a factor too, though over time we were steadily disabused of the notion. The friends we mentioned Ghent to now seemed all to have worked for institutions connected to the EU or to be—or partly be—Belgian. Or Dutch. It became a game for them to say to us, "Oh, Ghent, of course . . . " and then to rhapsodise about Liège or Namur or Durbuy. None of which we ever got to.

But I mention all this, why? I am not *in* Ghent, if that is what you are wondering. I haven't been back since. The reason is the news— which has seriously disrupted proceedings here, at the talks, as the group responsible for the attack has links to one of the sides to the negotiations. *Alleged* links, I should add; links that are vehemently denied. "You can't imagine we would countenance such an atrocity," Noor's expression seemed to say when he caught my eye in the corridor. "Not at such a critical time for our proceedings," he managed to add as I rushed past, head lowered, not to be swayed. It was he who stepped aside at the last moment. Having got his point across. I was on my way in to a one-to-one with his chief, the ambassador, Sabbagh. We have been at Gold Level throughout the day: a sign of the seriousness.

It started with the other party—with breathtaking cynicism (Sabbagh is right about that)—declaring that they would be withdrawing for the day as a mark of respect for the dead. "The martyrs of Ghent," they called them—which sounded like the title of another altarpiece, I mused at a low point. Not entirely appropriately, perhaps. They have been holding a vigil in their prayer room, though not saying prayers as such, I am advised. Apparently, Muslims are forbidden to pray for the souls of non-believers. Did Noor hold to this offensive injunction? I wondered. Probably not. Though my next thought was to enjoin myself to stop wondering what Noor might be thinking. What mattered was his party's line, which has been that continuing with the talks, getting on with the business of peace-making, is the more respectful response—a response that is of course as self-serving as the other party's withdrawal, however much I might personally sympathise with it.

Fifty-nine killed. Another eighty-eight injured. Not the highest number of casualties we have seen in recent years, but the very fact that we are almost inured to carnage on this scale tells its own story. It was one of these lorry attacks—in this case, two lorries, ploughing into a political rally staged by a right-wing party. The party leader is known for his vehement anti-immigrant views, and he and his followers are not—to say the least—the most pleasant people in the world, though that is hardly to the point and certainly no justification. As it happened, he—De Smet—and most of the senior figures in the party escaped unhurt. The casualties were overwhelmingly ordinary supporters, curious bystanders or incurious passers-by—or indeed, counter-demonstrators. Even so, you can imagine how this is playing politically across the continent.

Sabbagh has been insistent throughout the day that the group which has claimed responsibility for the incident is no longer an ally. "The alliance we briefly had with them was always a loose one anyway," he added. "But at a certain point, as you know, Mr. Behrends, the regime was crushing us; the situation was critical. How do you say it? We were a ragtag army—opposition forces, various separatists and, yes, religious militants, without a unified command, and bound only by most desperate circumstance."

The information I was receiving through the day suggested that the alliance was not only stronger than Sabbagh suggested, but more intact. What was less clear was the extent to which the attack was in fact directed by the militant group in question. The drivers of the lorries, both of whom were shot dead close to the scene, were identified as local boys, Brussels-born and radicalised—"home-grown terrorists," as they say. "Mr. Behrends, who I know is a student of his continent's history," Noor chipped in. He had joined the early-evening session, but not contributed much, it must be said. "Mr. Behrends will recall the alliance between Great Britain, the United States, and Stalin's Russia to defeat a common enemy, the greater evil, Nazi Germany. Sometimes.'

"Yes, yes, yes," Sabbagh interrupted with untypical brusqueness. He had judged—rightly—that Noor drawing this parallel at this time was not likely to be well received by me. Noor, a little shaken, withdrew from the exchange—a nod of the head; a stiffening of the back. He had clearly overreached himself. Quite right, I thought. This correction was overdue. Something of the proper order had been reestablished. Noor needed to remember I was much the more senior figure, a diplomat of repute and longstanding. There had been too much of this sense—just a slight pulse in the air between us—that we were equal partners in some sort of joint enterprise. Or at least, two men who understood each other in a way that others didn't. But he was wrong about that. I had continued to chair these talks with the most scrupulous even-handedness. There was no special closeness between me and Noor. And if I had given him that impression, that was a lapse on my part. "The point is, Mr. Behrends," Sabbagh continued, addressing me directly, "we have long repudiated all the activities of these terrorists. They are butchers and barbarians. All that is happening here is that the regime . . . "

We worked all day on a form of words; something

Sabbagh's leader, back in the region, could put his name to. It was a process not made easier by the most unhelpful statement from the other side rushed out in the immediate aftermath of the attack. That and this vigil of theirs was a destabilising move, I felt. By withdrawing for the day, they had pushed us into a proximity with the other side, thereby upsetting the exquisite balance of the talks. The absence of one side and not the other became more and more uncomfortable. We shouldn't have worked all day on something for Noor's leader, I realised too late in the day. The other side, the regime side, had played their hand more cleverly, I began to think. Though, in truth, I didn't know what to think—except that I had handled things very badly.

And all the time, I was thinking of Ghent. Not so much about the people of Ghent, or the victims of the attack, but of the Vrijdagmarkt, and of other squares, and of bridges and streets and canals and cafés. I was remembering places dear to us, in other words, and thinking how my precious perception of them had been disturbed, and perhaps for ever altered. Not in a foundational sense, but there would be that slight re-ordering of my thoughts about Ghent from now on. There would just be a beat in which this terrible terrorist incident came to mind before anything else. Before I recalled our many happy times there, before I thought of you and me together, which was all, really, that Ghent meant for us.

This must sound most self-absorbed, and, late in the day, when I watched a television report for the first time, my thoughts did extend beyond "our Ghent," as it were, and indeed beyond the ramifications for the talks. The TV corre-spondent used an obvious framing device: top-and-tailing his report with the story of a five-year-old Turkish girl, Elif—"lit-tle Elif," as she quickly became known—who was the first named fatality, and the youngest.

An immigrant Muslim child killed by Islamic extremists

targeting an anti-immigrant rally: the point was not lost on us. Nor the irony, if irony it was. We knew we were being manipulated. But we were moved nonetheless. (And I say "we" because I saw tears in the eyes of all my team—hardened as they are—as we watched this TV report together in the hotel lounge.) Indeed, this element of manipulation was essential to release emotion in us. Up until then, the enormity of the attack was such that we could not process it, and anyway we immediately channelled the anger and fear and sorrow it generated into dealing with the geopolitical consequences. We were lucky to have that outlet, in some ways. We could tell ourselves that we were working so that "some good would come from this tragedy", that we were helping to create conditions in which it would "never happen again", that we were building a peace that would be "a lasting memorial". Just such bromides were being spouted by politicians and civic leaders in Ghent and far beyond. Same tactic: deflection. But it doesn't do to deflect deep feeling for too long. This is another thing Caroline taught me.

It was welcome, then, that the atrocity had been reduced in dimension, packaged, to the size of a five-year-old, a huggable little thing, kitted out—in the photograph that had been released of her—in a woolly bobble hat, a bright anorak and a Peppa Pig rucksack. Rendered thus, the horror was bearably unbearable. A sliver of the parents' grief, rocking us for a moment—that dry gulp, that abysmal shudder—but releasing us back on the other side, where sadness is sweetness, stirring proof of common humanity, almost feel-good.

You? No, you were not brought up today, as you are not most days, though today the non-mentioning was the more studied for being top-of-mind. Exquisite and literal pains were taken. Lines in the forehead; a tightness around the eyes: these intended to make clear to me that I, you, we were in their thoughts, their prayers even, but they would never do anything so crass as to . . . Though Noor, right at the end of proceedings, started to say something. "Could I just say personally . . . " What desperation was this? Again, Sabbagh cut him short, whether sensing or not. Noor's humiliation was complete. Worse for him might follow. I took a savage delight in that. The day needed an injection of malice on my part. Any inclination to softness would have finished me.

Noor's own wife—admit it; you are expecting me to say: died in an air strike or was blown up in a car bomb?—is still living. The file on Noor is not specific about where; she has been at various times in Damascus, Amman, Cairo, Tunis. She is, like you, a medical doctor. In paediatrics rather than psychiatry. Noor himself is a doctor of philosophy. Degrees from the American University of Beirut, Sciences Po, the King Abdulaziz Center for World Culture. He and his wife met at the first of these. There is not a single extant photograph of her, which is surprising and lends her mystery—probably undeserved. If she were a "subject of interest," a drone or satellite image of her could have been obtained, wherever she is in the world, prior or not to her elimination.

These files: do they have something similar on us? Of course they do. We are all looking for any vanities or foibles. Where to probe. What to massage. What do they have on me? I wonder. It is all part of the psychology of this game. That I want to know. That I can't just look myself up. That I know what I know about them but don't know what they know about me.

I have neglected to mention it until now, but I have not neglected to think it: for every one of our Ghents, they have endured hundreds. They have Friday markets that have been attacked not just once, but multiply. Where the stalls are set up each day, amid uncleared rubble, on stones baked brown with blood, almost in expectation of a suicide attack or a massive car bomb. Then the funerals are attacked and the emergency services attending these funerals are attacked. Dead piled upon dead piled upon dead. Cries of grief becoming calls for revenge becoming cries of grief. And on and on it goes. They have their Annas too. (Not Noor, but several of the members of both delegations have lost wives.) And armies of little Elifs . . .

Ah now, have I betrayed myself? Armies: is that the appropriate word? Am I at some level thinking of armies with bombs packed into their Peppa Pig rucksacks? Am I at some level thinking their dead matter less than our dead? Is that it, Mr. Behrends?

Yes, there is something in that, Dr. Noor, as you insist on the point. It is why I resist so strenuously any exercise in equivalence. To take the instance you yourself have raised: children as perpetrators as well as victims. We would never sink so low. There are lines we do not cross. There are moral differences that at times amount to a gulf. Though that is not to say that we are not implicated, even where we are not directly involved, through alliances, proxies, arms sales, diplomatic failures, histories stretching back. We are implicated by dint of being human. The pathogen is species-wide and infects us all. That is why we are here.

War may now seem unimaginable on our old continent, but just think, what wars to get here! Wars of such destruction, atrocity and chaos! Wars of such virulence that finally, after centuries, millennia, and the one last hemoclysm—and that after a war to end all wars—we seemingly immunised ourselves against war. At most the odd outbreak in sixty, seventy years. The Balkans, the Ukraine. Nothing central to the nervous system of Pax Europaea. But then, who is to say this new normal will last? *The End of History*—remember that? Fukuyama has never lived that down. I went to a talk by him in Davos last year. He had a new book out, but no one was very interested in that.

In the meantime, we have found this other thing to occupy ourselves with. The *business* of peace. Brokerage and arbitrage. Whenever there is war elsewhere in the world—and there is no shortage; we make sure of that—we offer our services. Suave representatives of the savage protagonists are invited over and quarantined in luxury. Our best resorts, once sanatoria for the treatment of tuberculosis and other chronic diseases, are now sanatoria for the treatment of war. Our magic mountains, we trust, will cast their convalescent spell. The waters of our spa towns will be psychosomatically curative.

The picture I have in my mind is of an austere and monumental grey stone building; clerical in character, a seminary or the refectory of a monastery, perhaps? Two lines of Gothic arched windows, the lower line taller and more sculpted than the line above. A steeply pitched and tiled roof, punctuated with projecting roof windows. The mass of the building rising out of and reflecting in the black of the canal. A door with steps down to water level; those same steps leading back up to water level. A mirror image. There is no boat. And there are no lights in any of the windows. The evocation is deliciously sinister—a bat flits out of one of the windows, perhaps—certainly somewhat mysterious.

That was not the whole of it, of course. The building is artfully lit to create this effect. Indeed, the whole medieval quarter is illuminated in this way—see the Ghent Light Plan, first designed in 1998 and the winner of numerous prizes. Many other cities have followed suit. This is a city as a stage set, a brilliant fake: the Dark Ages subtly electrified. See also any number of restorative cleanings and repointings. Frontages re-rendered as they never were.

And when we are placed in the picture, you will see that we are walking back to the hotel from "our" restaurant, hand in hand, pleasantly drunk, mildly horny. I think it is early spring. A pleasantly warm day, but a distinct nip in the late-evening air.

A very comfortable bed, in a slightly overheated room, awaits us. We will probably pass on the sex but will sleep deliciously. Almost post-coitally. Perhaps in the morning we will be more in the mood. Perhaps not.

The waiter has just returned with my dry martini and a little bowl of salted cashew nuts. I thank him. His name is Anton, I believe, though I do not thank him by name. I have never been the type to do that. Maybe that is a pity, but there it is. I won't change now.

I am in the bar, if you're wondering. Yes, *again*. I have managed to nab the chesterfield by the great open fire. Cruickshank claims his room at his university hall of residence (he went to Exeter) was rather smaller than this fireplace, which might almost be described as "walk-in." The woodpile outside the hall is taller than a man and runs along an entire end of the building. Whole tree trunks are hauled down the mountain using chains and a sled and a snowmobile. Then men set to work with chainsaws. We hear the noise during the sessions. Those metal teeth tearing through wood flesh.

I was late to the mind-cleansing exertion of chopping wood. Gladstone was a great advocate of it, I read, in the excellent Jenkins biography I also have with me. Up in Urke in summer I lay in my own stockpiles of logs; far more than I will ever use in winter. One day someone will assume ownership of the cabin and the woodpile with it. Note that I don't say inherit. That thought hits me hard for a moment. But at the same time, the neat gin hits the spot. With that discordant hint of the savoury that the olive infuses. I know already that I will drink too much this evening, but what the hell! It's been a hell of a day. Sitting here with my martini by the fire is to be in a good place, however. The lap of luxury, one might say. And the sweet smell of woodsmoke is immensely calming. What type of wood is it? Some species of mountain fir, I suppose.

I find I am thinking about you without any great anguish. I

am missing you, but I am not lacerated by the thought. I have the drink to thank, no doubt. This is why I drink. For the blur and swim. A sharp mind is a razor's edge. Let me sink into befuddlement, will you. Let me recall in the blur and swim a Ghent that never was, but meant so much.

GOOD MAN

He was wearing a military-style greatcoat, theatrically long, its hem, sodden from the slush on the pavements, sweeping the floor. The slight young woman at the front desk relieved him of it and reeled under its weight. A colleague had to help her hoist the coat on to one of the brass hooks in the red-curtained cloakroom area, where it steamed like a racehorse in the winning enclosure.

Max, meanwhile, was unwinding what looked like a hand-knitted scarf and may well have been—hand-knitted, that is—though doubtless it was bought from a designer boutique at great expense even so. Who, after all, could you imagine knitting for him? Perhaps you, once. When you were a girl. No one since. The young woman put the scarf over her arm and waited while he removed his flat cap, which was one of those bigger, baggier Depression-era caps, this particular one made out of a patchwork of loud checked tweeds. Before handing it over, he made a show of thwacking the cap against his thigh to dislodge the covering of sleety snow from its crown.

Silver droplets cascaded on to the large red doormat of the restaurant, which was inlaid with its name—*Operzimmer*—in gold-coloured bristles. As a final flourish, he reached into his jacket pocket and pulled out a huge handful of coins, which he clattered into the brass tips plate.

It was quite an entrance, then; the entrance that Max knows is expected of him these days, having created that expectation himself over many years. Heads had turned at all of the tables nearer the door. And he was not done.

"Ed-VARD!" he bawled, spotting me suddenly—or pretending to—sitting on my own at a prominent table, big enough for six. (He had booked the table, and we were dining *à deux*, as far as I knew.) He then punched the air in triumph like the rider of that racehorse in the winner's enclosure and did a little jig on the spot. Now the whole restaurant was looking at Max, marvelling, thinking: Who on earth is that?

Then quickly: It isn't, is it?

(He was thirty minutes late for our lunch, incidentally. I didn't mention it and neither did he. And before you say anything, I was quite happy. I'd had an aperitif or two—and I had my book. *Bech at Bay*, as you insist. Not that I wasn't looking forward to seeing Max. It is always an event.)

The first thing to mention about him is that he was heavily bearded, which very much suited him, I must say, even though it made him look a decade older than his fifty-six years, the beard being predominantly and strikingly white. He was bulkier than when I last saw him too, and did not appear to be—*wasn't* would be a more precise way of putting it—especially clean. (By now, he was at the table and had hauled me into a back-slapping man-hug.) He gave off the air—a pungent whiff of it—of a man who had just rolled out of another man's bed, leaving this other man's wife sleeping the sleep of a fully sated woman—which might very well have been the case, of course. Though the aroma wasn't quite that—or not *just* that.

Too much information?

Several people had recognised Max by this stage, and the next few minutes were taken up with him hauling them into gamey embraces, grabbing their phones off them and taking selfies—expertly, I might add. Each one was shown off delightedly by Max to all those clustered around us as if it was some sort of miracle: Look at this phone! It takes pictures! I've taken a picture! Look, isn't it a good one!

"Plenty of practice," he explained, when I observed that he had mastered a tricky skill there. (And yes, I will admit I have taken a few selfies myself. Me on the mountain; me in the main square: that sort of thing. Though I do sometimes ask myself, who am I taking them for? Who is going to look at them in years to come? Me, I suppose.) His big entrance complete, Max had settled down at the table and was studying the wine list. First upside down; then the right way up. It struck me as he did so that this explanation of his skill at selfies had allowed Max to demonstrate self-deprecatory charm while simultaneously drawing attention to his celebrity—and that this was typical of him. "On the other hand, I've almost forgotten how to sign an autograph," he added from behind the wine list. It was a huge, plump, red-leather performance containing what must have been forty pages of wines. (In the end, he decided against wine. For both of us, until I chirped up. I had a couple of large glasses of Riesling. He had a glass of milk.) "So, it's very much *plus ça change, plus c'est la même chose, n'est-ce pas?*"

It was also very Max somehow—and somehow lovable—that he delivered the famous epigram in full. The atrocious French accent added to the effect. He has never managed to pick up any of the major European languages despite living for periods of years in France, Italy, Germany, and Spain. All that's happened is that his English has become oddly accented, as if it isn't his first, his only, language.

"Said who first, incidentally?" he added, looking over another new adornment or affectation of his: reading glasses. Large tortoiseshell ones. Perfectly round.

"No idea."

"You'll never guess." Lovable again. I had already made clear I wasn't going to try. "Give up?"

I nodded. Childlike, that was it.

"Jean-Baptiste Alphonse Karr."

"Never heard of him."

"Precisely." He already had Alphonse Karr's Wikipedia page open on his oversized smartphone and was holding it up for me. "Read any of this lot?" He had scrolled down to a list of all Alphonse Karr's novels.

- *Sous les Tilleuls* (1832)
- *Une heure trop tard* (1833)
- *Vendredi soir* (1835)
- *Le chemin le plus court* (1836)
- *Geneviève* (1838)
- *Voyage autour de mon jardin* (1845)
- *Feu Bressier* (1848)
- *Fort en thème* (1853)
- *Les Soirées de Sainte-Adresse* (1853)
- *Histoires Normandes* (1855)
- *Au bord de la mer* (1860)
- *Une poignée de vérités* (1866)
- *Livre de bord* (1879–80)

"Nope."

"You and the rest of the world. But just look at this . . . " He scrolled back up the page. "Alphonse Karr founded a journal, he was an expert on floriculture and had a number of plants, notably dahlias and a species of bamboo, named after him, and he was 'devoted' to fishing. And he lived in Nice and died in Saint-Raphaël. So, although he's only remembered for one epigram—and by that, I mean the epigram is remembered rather than him—we shouldn't feel sorry for old Jean-Baptiste."

I enjoy it, I'll admit: Max's fame, that is. I wouldn't want to be in his place, but I like being a satellite to the star. Orbiting Planet Max is not unlike standing behind the world leaders when an accord is signed. One fantasises for a moment that people are thinking: who is that? He looks important. I bet he's the one who did all the work and should really be taking the plaudits—only to realise that no one is thinking in this way; that *I* don't think in this way in equivalent circumstances—and that this thought is a relief. Really, it is. Proximity to the big guy is enough. A vicarious, big I-am.

He intuits all this, your brother, and this prompts him, semi-mischievously (I'm only semi-reluctant, after all), to drag me into the spotlight from time to time. He was at it at the launch party that evening.

"Here's the really important member of the family," he said, introducing me to somebody who had no interest in meeting me, however important I was, which they doubted quite frankly, but who had to put up with it because Max was doing the introducing, and being with Max, being *seen* with Max, was why they were here, as Max well knew, so put up with it they jolly well would. "I'm the hellraiser in the family," he continued, "while Ed here is the peace-maker."

As you can imagine, Max was especially delighted with this formulation of his. He trotted it out repeatedly as the evening wore on.

"Sandrine, ducky, darling! Sandrine, this is my brother-in-law, Ed." Sandrine—whoever she might have been: a buyer, a dealer, another artist, someone well known in this world, someone who, unlike me, palpably *belonged* in this world—extended a hand limply. "I'm the hellraiser in our family, while Ed here is the peace-maker." A titter from Sandrine or whoever. A polite enquiry of me as to what exactly it was I did do. Great relief when I brushed it aside. Even greater relief when I turned the conversation back to Max. "And anyway, let's not let Max deflect attention on his big day. Underneath it all, he's cripplingly shy, you know." A guffaw this time. My best moment. The *thank you, thank you*s that were going through the minds of the Sandrines at this point were almost visible on their lips. There they were thinking that they were going to be trapped with the bore of a brother-in-law for twenty minutes, only for the brother-in-law to save them from that fate—which made me somewhat less of a bore, perhaps, though they were not going to allow themselves to be caught out in this way. I understood why they really couldn't be expected to take any interest in me—not tonight anyway? their eyes said. Certainly, mine replied. Eyes being eloquent again.

"The problem with Ed, Sandrine," Max said, determined to be obtuse, "is that he is too self-effacing for his own good."

A look of alarm on the face of the Sandrine once more. We had dealt with this, hadn't we? Nobody wanted to discuss me; not even *I* wanted to discuss me, didn't Max get that?

I helped out by laughing. A thought had occurred—a rather neat one, if I say so myself. Self-effacing I might be, but not *too* self-effacing, surely. For, in truth, being self-effacing is the main thing, perhaps the only thing, I am good at. People often ask me . . . Let me rephrase that: I am occasionally asked . . . what is it exactly that I do? And on such occasions, they, the people asking me, are not asking, Sandrine-style, out of bare-minimum politeness; these people know I am a peace negotiator and are genuinely interested to find out what that entails. (There are such people.) And yet my answer generally takes the form of a self-effacing remark. "As little as possible," for instance. Or "Listen. Try to keep the show on the road. A prompt here, a prod there." Something of this sort. There is a certain flippancy about these remarks, for sure, but at the same time an essential truth. For, to a large extent, the art, the skill, the trick, in peace negotiations is to make it seem as if the deal is all the work of the two warring parties, that they have negotiated themselves to a settlement without any external intervention. What I am good at then—I realise I am making much the same point more or less—is getting something done without apparently having done anything very much. And while they don't present prizes for such work, there would be no prizes without it. I've sat in the front seats at the *Rådhuset* in Oslo, after all. Been mentioned by name on the White House lawn. Which is quite a proud boast, and risks undoing all of the above, which is why I would never say any of this to anyone—other than you, that is. Self-effacing for my own good, you see.

Meanwhile the Sandrine had, apparently successfully, moved the conversation on to a different subject, though it was also apparent that she/he/they were far from retaining Max's full attention, as all the while he, not to be denied his fun, was hunting the crowd with hungry eyes for his next victim . . . *Aha!*

"Günter! Günter, you absurd cunt. Günter, now you know I'm a bit of a hellraiser, well, here . . . "

A word about the space. Having exhausted the possibilities of housing art galleries in disused power stations or piano factories or synagogues or abattoirs, this one was housed in a disused art gallery. And before you say it, no, that doesn't just mean an old gallery refurbished and reopened as a new one. Or not quite. For the original gallery, in its derelict state, had apparently been left untouched, though that "apparently" is an important caveat. In fact, the dereliction had been carefully maintained, even added to and touched up somewhat. For instance, by hanging artfully vandalised paintings (defaced with graffiti, the frames broken; that sort of thing) on the damp-streaked, bubbled and blistered walls, and repositioning a smashed-up ornamental fountain so that the snow coming through a broken skylight collected in it. There was no heating in the building, I should add, and lighting was provided by flaming torches. There were vats of glühwein and a boar roasting on a spit. Max's greatcoat and scarf and cap—with added earmuffs—were perfect for the setting. Most of the women were in furs. Fun furs, funky furs, though I'm sure I got a whiff of fox and mink too. I was both underdressed for warmth and overdressed for smartness.

I won't try to describe the work Max was displaying. I know I'm Jim in the song: the only one in step, not just among the guests at launch parties, but among the public too. All I will say is that Max's real genius, in my view (I know, you've heard this a hundred times), is that he gets away with it. Still. Through sheer force of personality—that winning, generous, *lovable* personality; the truly great thing about him.

To give Max his due, he makes no claims at all as to the meaning, the point or the merit of his work. It is what it is, is his consistent—his smart—response to any requests for eluci-dation. I suspect—okay, I *know*—he suspects (or knows) what I think of it and so his generosity towards my work is the greater still. And my own supposed humility has a rather tinny ring to it. In the self-importance stakes I am the winner of the paper crown. After all, which of the two of us has five one-man shows running in four continents at the same time; which of us is being followed around by a TV documentary crew?

To return to the *Operzimmer*: it was, as I had suspected, just Max and I at our big table. And apropos of the documentary, the director didn't think Max having lunch with his brother-in-law was worth filming. "A welcome break," Max explained with a laugh when, his having told me about the film, I noted the absence of the crew. "It's been getting so I'm sitting on the pot, mid-dump, I look up, and the cameras are rolling."

See, self-deprecation and "I'm a celebrity" rolled up in one little phrase.

But the whole hellraiser/peace-maker number *was* per-formed for the cameras at the launch party, along with Max doing that affectionate headlock and hair-messing routine on me. I emerged from it red in the face and hair sticking up, looking like a fool. I hate it when he does this to me, but I dutifully played along, smiled gamely, essayed a friendly punch in the stomach that failed to land in every sense. Not to play the game makes you look a bigger fool. As would saying you would rather not be filmed at all, thank you very much.

Not that I was inclined to. For I am part of Max's story—a not-uninteresting sidebar, with that added element of "who-would-ever-have-guessed-those-two-were-related." I know that people like that Max and I are such contrasting characters, so I did the interview "in character," as it were—the plodding diplomat rather bemused by his charismatic artist brother-in-law. I have no illusions as to how little I will feature in the eventual film. The only purpose I will serve is as a bridge to the heart of Max's story: the episode in which his sister was brutally murdered. Max will have talked at some length about the attack, about his struggle to cope with the loss. But he will have not made it all about him; he will have tried to turn it back to you—your brilliant career cut short. I will get a mention too. My grief. My loss. And Max's display of grief will be heartfelt. Without setting out to, he will emerge well from the episode, I have no doubt. Viewers will see a more vulnerable side to him and his popularity will grow even greater. Though on his beloved social media there will also be a backlash—people accusing him of exploiting personal tragedy to enhance his celebrity. He will show dignity and restraint in the face of these accusations; win more plaudits; attract more opprobrium. He can't win and he will win. This is the way of things, these days. I know it from my own much lower-wattage experience. Max is a master of art.

Does he keep up such a punishing schedule to fill the hole left by your death? There is something in that. The two of you—so very different in many ways—were always close. He was devastated by your death. The weight of him, a heaving sea on my shoulder, will stay with me for ever. That said, he always did drive himself hard. You don't get where he has got to unless you do. Still, five shows over four continents and all the rest . . . He looked shattered at times over lunch; the times when he wasn't putting on a public performance—and most of the time he wasn't. Indeed, I did most of the talking. He listened quietly, intently—sometimes distantly. Almost nodding off now and then, but otherwise giving every impression that he was interested in the progress of the talks, the wider geopolitical considerations, the people in my team, and all the other things I had been dying to tell someone about. It is touching, I thought with real warmth, that he always finds time for me when I call or email to suggest we meet up. Which I do sparingly, I should add, knowing the demands on his time.

I am in Austria, I had told him. Chairing talks in a mountain resort.

"Yes, you did tell me . . . "

But I was due some leave, and I saw that his one-man was opening, and I was planning to come to Berlin anyway at some stage, and so I was wondering . . .

"Of course," he started off, as ever, quite cautiously.

But then his enthusiasm ratcheted up.

"Come to the launch party." And up. "We'll have dinner. We'll go out on the town." And up. "This is great news. Good man!"

I remember hearing the words "good man" for the first time during my first proper cricket match at my first English boarding school. Another boy had been hit by a fast ball in the box, that most intriguing (to a half-Norwegian boy at least) piece of kit, a sort of plastic codpiece, which is worn inside the jockstrap (another wonder), to mitigate against the ill effects of just the eventuality that befell my teammate. Though "mitigate" is the word: it still hurt like hell. It was to happen to me later in the season. And on that occasion, as with the first one, the games master used the commendation "good man" to approve our relative bravery—our eyes were watering, but there was no actual crying—while at the same time suggesting that it was only to be expected of us. Personal goodness did not come into being a "good man," I realised. For "good man" was not a shortening of "you are a good man" but rather of "good, you are a man." In other words, "good" was not an adjective that attached to any individual because of their own virtue, but rather it attached to all men by virtue of their *being* men, assuming that they behaved in a suitably male way, which was very much to be assumed, hence the general approbation inherent in the expression.

There was a proviso, however, buttressed by the accent in which "good man" was then, and has always been, conveyed in my hearing; that is to say, the man behaving in a suitably male way, out of an innate sense that to behave in any other way would simply not do, was assumed to be an Englishman being an Englishman, rather than men in general conforming to type. And while there is a colossal national arrogance in this assumption, there is also a certain generosity in it too, I feel, because first on that cricket field, but also many times since, I have found that honorary English status can be conferred on any man who steps up to the mark, such that "good man" can also be read as "Good, you are a man, as is proved by your acting like an Englishman, which any man can do if he puts his mind to it."

All of which I instinctively warm to, for whatever you say about English maleness—and I sense you are poised to come up with quite a list—it has the virtue of not being aggressively macho, but rather is characterised by a certain restraint, an essential decency and a genuine—if self-regarding—sense of the ridiculous. It is in large part why I have, over the years, cultivated an English sensibility, albeit one that doesn't care for cricket (and not just because of that ball in the balls), and why, most of the time, I do not mind being taken for an Englishman—which, as can be imagined from this digression, happens often, even if it is, more and more, a disadvantage in the world of diplomacy. If not life in general.

I mention all this because, with conversation flagging at the lunch table, I embarked on just this extended riff on the meaning of the term "good man" to Max, who enjoyed it hugely—as I knew he would, he being an Englishman of just the type to do so, even though his other persona, that of rock star of the art world, might seem at odds with this disposition. (On managing that tension, by the way, think the members of the Monty Python team or "Sir" Mick Jagger.) I mention it also because of what Max said next.

"Ah, but you are a good man more generally, Ed," he said. "I'm always saying that to other people."

"I wish you wouldn't," I said, partly because I genuinely felt it, but also because what else could I say in the circumstances? I don't want to go back over the same ground, but if "good man" etiquette teaches you anything it is that you demur at any suggestion that you are a good man in the wider sense.

I should have said as much to Max as it would have punctured the sudden seriousness; it would have made him laugh. But I didn't think to. And so there we were, left smiling awkwardly at each other, if only for a moment.

"If you knew what I sometimes thought, what lurks inside, you certainly wouldn't say it—or think it," I went on eventually.

"Oh, that . . . " Max said. "Morose delectation. Old Aquinas. If that's sin then we are all in hell. What I mean is you have good intentions, you do good acts, you *get* to do good acts. Perhaps another way of putting it is, you are a lucky man."

"Now, there I would agree with you."

"Of course—" he added quickly, panic flaring in his eyes. He was about to explain. But I of coursed him back. Waved it away. For I am a lucky man. Lucky to have been lucky for so long, to still be so on so many counts. Can you imagine how I would have coped if I hadn't been?

At the launch, I excused myself as soon as I decently could, the non-demands of being Max's brother-in-law having worn thin as they always do. Max protested. I was to join "them" for dinner and then "who knows?" But I have spent a lifetime absenting myself from such open-ended evenings, regretting and yet not regretting it. It's not me; it can't be or I wouldn't keep doing it. Have I missed out on a lot of life? No doubt. Could I have lived differently? I haven't.

Max hauled me into another man-hug before letting me go. He smelt better: of paraffin, of smoke, of the roasted skin of wild boar, of the most expensive women's perfume. Perhaps there was even paint in there somewhere. Turps. It was a heady mixture, anyway.

It will be another few months before we meet again and who knows where that will happen? Do either of us even know where the other one is living these days? And I don't mean the actual address, I mean the city, or even the country. I think he is "based" in Helsinki. But also "has homes" in New York and Chile. I may be wrong. Apart from my old Aunt Else, in Alesund, Max is my one living relative. (I'm not counting cousins I haven't seen for fifty years.) As I was driven back to my hotel through the frozen city, I thought about that and I was strangely content that it was so. How many more times will we see each other? If it was twice a year for the next twenty years, our meetings would number forty. Quite enough. I will look forward to them in advance, talk about them to friends afterwards, but not enjoy them as much at the time. Not feel entirely comfortable, at least.

I almost forgot. He had that son. The past tense seems right somehow, for all that the "boy" is very much alive. I don't believe Max has seen him in many years. I certainly haven't. Did you see him a year or two before your death? I should remember. Max didn't mention him anyway. And I didn't bring him up. But he is out there somewhere, still living with his mother in France or the United States—or perhaps not. He'd be eighteen or nineteen now. He could be at university or film school or art college. Christoph, then: I have one more relative—of a sort—than I thought I had only moments ago. Did he come to your funeral? (I don't remember much of that day.) Now I think of it, I think he did.

Well, he certainly won't come to mine.

N ext day I had the usual round of meetings with ministers and officials. I mention these even though I have nothing to say about them: they were routine, useful in their way, satisfactory on the whole. As with the merry-go-round of summits, conferences and bi-laterals I also attend, the main purpose of these meetings is to keep meeting, to keep talking. We meet so we can meet again. Talk again. It might seem nothing much, nothing at all, is achieved by all this meeting. We, more than anyone, are oppressed by this thought. But just consider for a moment what happens when these meetings stop.

Pregnant pause.

What?

(You're back then.)

No, tell me.

(It's as if you never went away.)

I give up.

Okay, the future of the human race doesn't hang on them. Much of the diplomatic round is about maintaining the diplomatic round. And now I am repeating myself. But . . .

Some of these dull meetings are quite important. They help to end wars, to keep the peace. We get it. Keep it up.

It was often observed that you were not the typical diplomat's wife. Though never more than once in your hearing.

"You see, Kevin, that is at best a dubious compliment to me, while at the same time downright offensive about other wives and partners . . . "

But let me tell you what I wanted to tell you.

As I was walking from one ministry to another, up Unter den Linden, it occurred to me that I never pay much, indeed any, attention to the linden trees themselves. It being winter, the trees were not in leaf. But I have walked down the famous boulevard many times, in spring, summer and autumn, and while appreciating that it is tree-lined, and certainly that it is named after its trees, the lindens have always passed me by, so to speak. The thought led me to make a close inspection of them this time. Of their bark, of the pattern of the branches, of the structure of the trees against the background of a leaden sky. I can't say I found the exercise very interesting for long. Within a minute or two, the intense cold and the need to get to my next meeting in good time provided me with the excuse to resume my walk.

When I told Martin, the deputy foreign affairs minister, about this incident he laughed and told me a story. Apparently, Hitler had the linden trees cut down in 1936 and replaced with smaller trees which wouldn't, as the lindens had, obscure the giant Nazi flags. There was such a public outcry, however, that he had to back down and have the lindens replanted.

It was my turn to laugh. "The lesser-known side of the Führer," I said. "The one ready to say, "Hey! Hands up, I got it wrong.""

Martin looked troubled. I hadn't meant it in this way, but it struck me that my remark must raise the thought in a German that if public pressure had saved the lindens then why had so little been exerted to save the Jews? I regard Martin as a friend; someone I can talk to frankly. But we have only once discussed the degree of culpability of the German people for the rise of Nazism, for the devastation of a continent, for the Holocaust. We had been enjoying a light-hearted lunch at a little lakeside place in Wannsee and had got through a couple of excellent bottles of Piesporter when the subject came up. Martin's mood darkened dramatically. Such was the ferocity with which he denounced the conduct of his grandparents" generation that I was almost moved to defend them. His grandfather had been a customs and excise official, I recall, and so necessarily a member of the Nazi Party. But there was no suggestion that he had been anything other than one of those good men who do nothing. No hero certainly, but then how many of us are? Personally, I am not in the least confident that in the same situation I would have acted differently—risked Dachau or the piano wire. Was Martin so certain he would? I doubted it. But then he is a German, a senior German politician moreover, and as such could not be seen to show the slightest empathy towards his grandfather for fear of how that would look to me, a non-German diplomat, albeit a friend.

It is the burden all his fellow countrymen and women carry—not unreasonably, perhaps. Martin would certainly never complain, for all that he would like to be rid of this guilt by association. You, I remember, felt no twenty-first-century Briton should ever suggest that the evils of empire, of the slave trade, and all the rest, have nothing to do with them. There is no sloughing off all the dead tissue, you felt; no pretending that a new generation emerges clean-skinned, unstained by the sins of fathers and grandfathers. "And mothers and grandmothers," I suggested teasingly. "Them too," you conceded sulkily. Part of our work, for all that we must look forward and live in our own time, is due reparation for the misdeeds of our forebears, you continued. Not useless shame, but active recompense. Not direct financial compensation, perhaps—though we might argue about that—but fairer trade deals and greater access to markets, and certainly due respect and parity of esteem in international affairs.

Martin—now rather uncomfortably—was sitting behind his huge, dark wood desk, in his high-ceilinged office, double doors leading to a balcony that Martin had told me on a previous visit he only once had stepped on to. It was the sort of balcony from which a politician might wave to crowds of supporters chanting his name in the street below, I had observed. There you are then, Martin had responded drily. Heavy net curtains, made of a soft metal mesh material designed to stop glass being blown inwards in the event of a bomb explosion nearby, hung in front of the double doors. One of the things we discussed was the threat of such an atrocity. After Ghent there was much nervousness across Europe. There had been several arrests in Berlin in recent days.

I had spent the day in grand public buildings like this one. I had entered through columned porticos and waited in marble halls with frescoed ceilings. I had been ushered down endless corridors, their walls hung with portraits of nineteenth-century statesmen or panoramic battle scenes.

Or all was glass and freakish palms, walls of sheet water and carelessly commissioned abstraction, bullet lifts shooting up through the inevitable atrium. There were buildings too in which the shell of the old contributed to the new vernacular—stripped back, reclaimed, an eye for flaw and imperfection. In this city of successive twentieth-century nightmares, the German architect has the smashed and blackened brick of bomb and conflagration, bullet holes from street fighting, the scratched messages of political prisoners, the daub of ideological graffiti, the ghost of a deported race, to work with if he dares.

Then there are the mausoleums of the old GDR to which a certain institutional stink clings for all their incorporation into, and reinvention by, the new Germany. The young Turk knows how to play with the grim ironies to achieve maximum frisson. There is none of that in London or Paris, never mind Geneva or Stockholm. I couldn't live here for this reason, for all that I love to visit.

But I mention the grandness of the buildings only to make

the point that they impress so little on proceedings. A meeting in a mirrored stateroom or mosaicked palazzo is just another meeting. Sometimes I do look up into a domed ceiling or vaulted hall and try to soar. But something—the hardness of my chair, a man over there sneezing, a trivial and irrelevant thought—always brings me down to earth. Is it any different for world leaders, for great—or supposedly great—men or women? Quite probably. And the thought is rather alarming if anything. Better to be a modest man dwarfed by the immensity of the task, doing his best, failing more often than not. These cathedrals to power should not delude one as to one's importance.

On the expanse of desk, facing Martin but just visible to me, was a framed photograph of his wife and young children. His second go at it. In conformity to the modern way, Martin has changed a lot of nappies this time around. He makes a point of getting home for the family evening meal. He reads bedtime stories.

He says he enjoys it.

"You don't, I'm told," Martin said. "Have children, I mean."

This was at a drinks party in New York soon after we were first introduced. We were both attending something UN-related. I can't remember what now.

"No, that's right," I said.

One of the reasons I was drawn to Martin was that he showed such frank curiosity about our not having children.

"I find them interesting, that's all," he continued, reaching across to take a piece of chicken satay on a bamboo skewer from a passing waiter. "Childless couples."

I will risk it: there's a German bluntness about Martin. You would say I was guilty of crude stereotyping, but his straightforwardness seems typically German to me. It is not unfriendly. In his case anyway. Quite the opposite, in fact.

"They seem odd to me."

By now, I was laughing. Martin had finished his chicken satay and was looking around for a waiter on to whose platter he could deposit the bamboo skewer.

"Both times we—my wives and I—had children within a couple of years of meeting, never mind marrying."

The daughter from his first marriage has a serious eating disorder; one of the sons is a relatively famous actor. Martin is close to them now. And on amicable terms with his first wife, also an actor, despite her vocal opposition to the government of which he is a member. There is something quite German about all that too.

"Anna, my wife, never wanted them," I said.

This telling him outright—that it was you, not me, who didn't want children—was another sign somehow. Of my very much trusting and liking this Martin Frink fellow. Who was now accepting his third or fourth top-up from the wine waiter. Who was reaching out for another of the canapés: this time, strips of Oriental beef, with a sweet chilli sauce. The red plastic cocktail stick on which the beef was impaled resembled a tiny fencing sword, I recall. (Funny the minutest details one remembers at times. My recollection of the whole of this exchange is photographically precise.) Not spotting a passing platter on to which he could deposit the tiny red sword, Martin popped it instead into the chest pocket of his jacket. A few other cocktail sticks went that way as we talked. I remember thinking that these would only be discovered when the jacket went for dry-cleaning. For some reason that was a thought which made me sad.

"Agnostic" was the word I always used to describe my own view of having children, I told him. But you were certain we would enjoy a better life together without them.

"And did you?"

See what I mean about Martin?

"Yes, I think so. Of course, there is no counterfactual."

The significance of this exchange will not have escaped you. You can see why it stands out as being so important to me. For I know you haven't approved of my not making things as clear to others. In the many interviews I gave, for instance. Or when I am giving public talks, as I still do, though less frequently as time goes on.

My fear was that saying you never wanted children would make you seem less sympathetic somehow; rather cold and hard-hearted; rather overly focused on your career and your own pleasures. It is a deeply conventional view, no doubt, even a reactionary one, and I can hear you saying: *Well, for a start, that is deeply sexist. No man . . .* But it was why also—you will have to forgive me, this gets worse—I have tended not to refer to your quick temper, or that you were not very romantic, or indeed sentimental at all. It wasn't just children. You didn't much care for animals either. Or suffer fools—or charlatans—at all. Or have a high opinion—*Let's be frank, I had a low opinion*—of most of your fellow Britons. Of most people generally, for that matter.

But I loved you, darling.

I remember an interviewer in those early days saying that I must find Christmas a particularly difficult time, and I was reminded of your ambivalence—let's make that downright dislike—towards Christmas. (*Can we agree to a moratorium on buying each other presents again?*) The memory made me laugh out loud. The interviewer looked surprised and, in this instance, I did say, "The fact is Anna was not a great one for Christmas," and the interviewer looked sad, and I felt I must add, "But yes, I do miss her more at these special family times." *Traitor*, I could sense you snarling.

So, yes, I have been guilty of painting you, of memorialising you, and—as time has gone on—even remembering you, in softer tones than were true to the lived experience. With its

more barbed edges. With you in the room. Who did nag and irritate. Who did pontificate and *go on.* Who at times I couldn't stand. Who at times I wished would just . . .
Fuck off?
Quite.
It may seem strange but it is the memory of such exchanges that tears most keenly at my heart. You could be a bloody difficult woman (*and you could be a bloody difficult man.* Granted) but it is that woman—you—I miss the most. Perhaps I have contributed to the creation of a softer version—not you—for just that reason. It makes the public grieving—still a part of my life—easier to get through. I am remembering and honouring you at one remove. And I know you scorn and ridicule all that, but I will be attending memorial and named-in-your-honour events for some years to come, Anna Dupont. Like it or not, you were—or have become—a respected and almost loved figure in certain circles. It does sometimes make me laugh (and I have to put on a serious face because people look so taken aback) when I hear you described in these gatherings, as you often are, as "a believer in peace and reconciliation," as someone who "brought communities together," who was a "great healer." True, you were pioneering in your field; you improved, even saved, many lives; you campaigned for and spoke out about many causes, most notably on mental health issues; but gentle, pacific, conciliatory?
Tell me about it, I can hear you saying. *You're to blame, Ed; it was your handling of my death that has led me to be remembered in this way. If it had been me, I'd have been calling for them to rip* his *bloody head off . . .*
This is why Martin has been such a godsend: because from the start I have felt no pressure to portray you in any way other than the way you were. You would have liked him. He you. He often says as much.
"Did she like other people's children?"

"Not greatly."

"And didn't make a lot of effort to disguise the fact, I'd guess," he laughed. I laughed too. "I like the sound of this woman. My little ones would have adored her. There's no one they love better than an adult who couldn't care less about them."

I visited the Frinks' home the last time I was in Berlin. The house—a new-build—was one of those surprisingly modest homes that some quite senior people favour in certain northern European countries.

The little ones adored me too, I might add, though I am not quite such a stern challenge.

The toddler, Ruthie, said straight out, "Your mummy is dead."

"That's my girl," Martin laughed, appearing with the wine.

"His wife, not his mummy," the older one corrected.

"You can play with us, anyway," Ruthie said.

I was going to, but Martin hastened to tidy the children away. He left me with his wife, Fredda, while he did the bedtime thing. How much did we miss out? I sometimes wonder.

Let's not go there.

You again.

Probably best.

I moved the conversation in Martin's office on to the progress of the talks, what pressure the German government might apply behind the scenes, how things were seen in other capitals. We talked over sandwiches and coffee that were brought in. We had moved into the armchairs by the fireplace by this stage. The fire was not lit. Martin did suggest meeting for a drink in the evening. Fredda and the children were at Fredda's mother's house in Würzburg. But I was catching a flight. On to London, then Paris, then Geneva, then back to the mountain.

Later in the afternoon I walked up Unter den Linden one

more time. Sleet was now falling and a day of relentless grey was blackening into night. Again, I thought of how many times I had walked up this avenue over the years—and this time I remembered to include you in the reflection. How many times had *we* walked up this avenue, never looking at the trees after which it was named (that went for you too), but also—and this hit me harder—never making the connection. Are you with me?

I take it from your silence—and forgive my juvenile delight—that you haven't twigged, that I've stumped you—tree puns very much intended.

Unter den *Linden*. Den *Linden*.

Us doing the crossword together, do you remember? One of us working out a tricky clue and, instead of just telling the other the answer, saying—all smug now: "Oh, *of course.*" And the other one (more often than not me) saying: "It's no good saying 'of course' like that, as if it is obvious; you've been staring at it blankly for twenty minutes." And you (it was generally you) saying: "I wasn't staring at it blankly, I was studying it intently, and I can now see it *is* obvious. It was staring us right in the face."

And you would laugh at the expression on my face—not amused—and would start saying (or singing), to take one example: "Dinner, dinner, dinner, dinner, dinner, dinner, dinner, dinner . . . Eight times eight across serves up . . . " Still a blank look from me. The look from you: pure elation, pure triumph. "It doesn't get any better than this" was written all over your face. "BATMAN. Eight across is 'Dinner'. Eight times eight across is 'Dinner, dinner, dinner, dinner, dinner, dinner . . .'" "Okay, I get it. 'Batman'. Very clever." Your delight was such that you might almost have devised the clue, not just solved it. But here's the thing: as much as I was exasperated with you, as annoying as you were being—deliberately, provocatively—I loved you so much at moments like these.

(You can see a theme developing here.) And I loved so much being in the couple's closed circle. The tight, taut drum. Purely in and of itself, intrinsic to a fault.

So, have you got it yet? Nope. You're sulking. Still love you. Love you for ever. Perhaps I have been too hard on you today? Perhaps I have made both of us seem unlovable? Strange sort of love story, this, until you stop to think that we found each other. Not luckily, I like to think, but inevitably. It was nothing to do with fate or destiny. It was algorithmic. An equation that could only equal. An alignment that had to be. After all, who else would have had us?

The answer is: Philemon and Baucis. (Please don't say it was on the tip of your tongue. By rights, this is flat-of-the-hand-against-forehead time.) Philemon and Baucis: the greatest love story of all time; the story all lovers should yearn towards and aspire to. Granted one wish: to die at the same moment and so never to be parted. The linden tree entwined around the oak.

It was you who read it to me, remember? "The household consisted of two." In Ovid's version in *Metamorphoses*.

Sentimental old lovebirds after all. The fact that it is one of the great classical fables helped, no doubt. If it had been a Disney film it would have been a different matter. Though I also remember you mentioning that you were weary of books peddling their seriousness by reworking Greek myths. You're going to have to bear with me on this one then. Because, under the lindens, their naked branches standing out stark in the winter night, I found myself retelling the old tale. To myself.

There was this fellow, Phil, that's me, and his wife, Babs, that's you. They were poor (well, we were never rich rich), and they were good (that again; more good than bad anyway), and they were devoted (true, unequivocally), and they were happy (ditto—most of the time). In many versions of this tale it might have been said that the gods were smiling on them. But of course, Phil and Babs didn't believe in the gods. Or God singular. Or the fates or destiny. (We've dismissed all that already.) Or even in good luck. At least, not to the extent that it extended more readily to good people. Luck was a brute. Unevenly and unfairly distributed.

And before we continue, let's nail this good-people thing. Phil and Babs had once, for two months, a refugee stay in their house, in one of their two spare bedrooms. Good for them, surely? Not quite. The fact was they found the experience most unsettling. Indeed, let's turn that up a notch or two. They *hated* almost every minute of it. They wondered how it was that other people, friends among them, found putting up a refugee so rewarding, so uplifting. Frankly, they doubted these friends were being entirely honest about it.

The problem was he was always there. He didn't want to be in the way and they were hardly ever in. But whenever they were, there he was. Ezekiel, his name was. On the landing, in the kitchen, in the living room. Though much more often in his room. Hardly making a sound, but still in the house, *their* house.

The three of them shared a few (awkward) dinners together, but mostly Phil and Babs were out in the evenings. They led busy lives and found themselves busier still during those two months. They left early in the morning and returned late at night. Ezekiel had a key. He had the run of the house. He came and went. And finally—it was a long two months—went. For good. He left a thank-you note and a small bunch of flowers.

They wanted to hug each other, to dance a little jig for joy, when they found that note and read what it said. That at least was what they both felt separately—and had one of them acted on this impulse, they would surely have done it. For later—years later—they admitted this to each other and found it was not too late. Hugging each other and dancing around the kitchen—admittedly, drink-fuelled—as they remembered the

day poor Ezekiel left their home. Do these seem like good people to you?

Happy ending: a social housing tenancy had been secured
for Ezekiel by the refugee charity. A place of his own. No
doubt he was much more comfortable there than living in their
home. Though of course Ezekiel thanked them very much for
allowing him to stay and he hoped Phil and Babs would visit
him one day.

They didn't. And neither did they take in another refugee.
What they did do was triple their direct debit to the refugee
charity. There and then. The night Ezekiel left. They were
thanked in the quarterly newsletter. It proclaimed them
Patrons or Angels or something of the sort. They quickly dis-
posed of the quarterly newsletter. But the flowers Ezekiel left
behind as a token of his thanks bloomed seemingly for weeks.
It was a relief when they withered and died, when Phil and
Babs could finally chuck them out.

But here is the oddest part of their tale: Phil and Babs, for
all that they had no illusions about their goodness, about good
fortune and just deserts, *still* trusted that the fabled ending
would enfold around them. In their version, they would live
together into old age and then die, if not at exactly the same
moment, then within a year or two of each other. Pretty pain-
lessly and peacefully; accepting the end, happy they had had a
good life. And yes, an oak would be planted somewhere,
around which a linden would entwine. They had discussed
making it happen. Could a municipal cemetery or public park
be persuaded to do such a thing? For years after people would
read the plaque and nod their heads and smile and say, "Ah, a
real-life Philemon and Baucis." And Phil and Babs got a kick
out of that thought, not least because it meant they would be
recognised not just as a devoted couple, but a well-read one.
Who knew the classics, who knew their Ovid.

There is a twist, though. And not *that* twist. A twist that precedes and supersedes. The fact is, I—the one left behind; the one disabused, one might say—still believe that the story of Phil and Babs *should* have ended this way. No matter that it didn't. It would have been the more natural order of things— and so much more *plausible*. I cite any number of eminent reports and peer-reviewed papers showing ever-increasing longevity, rapid advances in medical science, improvements in palliative and end-of-life care, not to mention studies that prove that as we get older our fear of death reduces, such that we eventually wish for our end. We have every chance, we really do, that we will fade away with our loved one holding our hand, free of pain, free of fear, knowing he or she will follow soon after. We are white, Western, well-off, well-educated, living in the best districts of the most advanced cities in Europe in the twenty-first century—truly, for us, the story is supposed to end this way.

What stretches credibility so, what tips into the realms of the fabulous, is that a 55-year-old woman, a distinguished consultant psychiatrist, should leave a Central London research institute one afternoon in May, in the second decade of the twenty-first century, and be decapitated by a young, heavily bearded man, of "Middle Eastern" appearance, wielding a mighty sword and shouting "Allahu Akbar."

Off with her head, swish, gone, dead. Pouf! Like something out of *The Arabian Nights*.

How could that have happened? And to such good people.

To mention just one initiative, there are now hundreds of young women around the world who have benefited from Dupont scholarships. They write to me to say how inspired they are by your example. You did such good work. You were such a good person. And what a good person I am for creating the scholarships in your memory.

Yes, how weary one can grow of all this. The heavy mantle draped around our shoulders yet again. With the best of intentions, no doubt. But wouldn't we throw it off in an instant for just a few selfish minutes more? For a snatch of time together against the world? And in your case—don't deny it— the more pointed "me-time"? With me out of the picture. What would you give for that? All the good you did, I'd bet.

I was in a taxi to Tegel by this stage, looking out through lachrymose windows on a city in turns bleak and cold, light and warm. Black rivers, canals, and waterways. Dark hulks of industry and tenement. The dazzle of finance, consumerism and lifestyle. Pockets of domestic, almost cottagey warmth. This is a spread-out, strangely underpopulated city. For the moment my own pocket, this overheated taxi, is a comfort— as, later, my seat in the plane will be. And the luxury hotel room in London.

But to return to Phil and Babs one last time. Phil has been left on his own, then. Feeling foolish or betrayed—or a bit of both. Though, as we've seen, he *still* believes. And at this point in the tale—the crux of it—he is confronted with a terrible truth, already hinted at. What if their one wish could have been granted, but with this twist? That he too is cut down in the street. A second swish of the sword and he dies in almost the same instant alongside Babs. Never to live into ripe old age, but never to be parted from his beloved wife. Deal? asks Mephistopheles. (The tale has turned Faustian for some reason.) Or no deal?

I have arrived at the airport. Gone through security into the first-class lounge. I like this time before a flight starts boarding. I order a brandy from the barman. The thing is, there are comforts. The treacherous comforts of life.

One thing nobody has encouraged me to do is to start a new relationship. Indisputably "too soon, too much": we can all agree on that. I suppose at some point there will come a time. Though, having said that, I wonder if there ever will. One of those touching care-home romances, perhaps? Even then . . .

For a start, I am still in a relationship with you. That relationship has suffered the most grievous shock and yet I am as committed to it, as intensely in love, as I have ever been. More so, in fact. What is going to change that? People say time—though thankfully never to me. I have found time to be a thin diluting agent. Or rather, it works to purge raw grief but at the same time bathes and beautifies and beatifies love. Steeps and essentialises it. What remains is a perfect distillation; love in its purest form—100 per cent proof.

Not then the healthiest form?

I can hear you adding the qualifier. And here's the paradox: more than anyone it is you I can most imagine urging on me a new relationship—*not now . . . but in due course.* Whatever that might mean? *Look it up, why don't you.* (See, we are squabbling in that way we so enjoyed.) And yet—here's the paradox again—remembering and so missing you in this irritating form is just what will stop me, give me pause.

Aha! Weakening already.

But I raise this business of a new relationship, why? Given that I appear to have done so only to dismiss it out of hand. I suppose part of it is that it has allowed me to make these declarations of—forgive me—undying love. I have been reflecting on the implications of the story of Phil and Babs, my "Unter den Linden" moment. But also, while I was in London—for the briefest stopover—I had what might be termed a "date."

And having said that, albeit qualified by those quotation marks, let me correct myself. (Why do I keep doing this?) For the word "date" was certainly not used, or even implied, either by our friend Jean, who suggested I might like to meet up with her friend Josephine, or by Josephine herself, who was my dining companion. Dinner was the word used. Not even dinner date. And there was no sense among the parties to it (I include myself emphatically) that if the dinner went well, sex, romance, a relationship would come of it at some point. If not there and then—nothing so vulgar as that—then "in due course," perhaps. And that is what a "date" implies. At least it does to me. Am I wrong? Ignoring your grin, I consult my much-thumbed *Shorter Oxford*: "An appointment or engagement at a particular time (esp. with a person of the opposite sex)." I am wrong. Or am I? I think we can agree that a tantalising dot dot dot is left dangling off the end of this entry? All of which is neither here nor there in this instance, however, because we are not talking about a date. That is the point we have, somewhat tortuously, arrived at.

I do this sometimes, I have noticed: imply awkwardness where none exists save for my implication of it. It avoids greater awkwardness further down the road, is all I can say for myself. But that doesn't alter the fact that I arrived at the restaurant a bundle of excruciation. I conveyed it in every knotted fibre of my being. That was clear from Josephine's elaborately wrought manner towards me. She was immediately and ever at pains. Fastidious to a fault in avoiding any possibility of misunderstanding. Not that we did. Either of us.

Misunderstand. We understood perfectly. Where we stood. The nature of this evening, that is.

She kept this . . . this . . . this . . . up all evening. I played my part, but this was my first time. She had been here before. It must have been immensely wearying. Why had she agreed to this dinner? I kept thinking.

But then, why had I?

A word about the restaurant. Though Jean had played matchmaker, as it were, I was not staying with her and John, which I often do. And for some reason none of our other friends was able to accommodate me. Which was fine. I was only in town for a night on business so I put up in a hotel. For reasons that I don't need to explain, I was not about to invite Josephine to dine at the hotel, even though it has an excellent restaurant. But I might have booked a hundred and one different places, some of which—before you jump in: *Not one of our favourites, surely?*—I have eaten at, or come to like, or have even opened, since you died.

Stop.

The thought floors me. This is happening more and more, of course. Places, events, experiences that separate us in space and time—me here and now and you . . . where, when? So far away, suddenly. And for ever. Out there. Nowhere. Worlds devoid. You don't exist in any of them. You don't exist at all in any sense that means anything to me. *All this?* Is just conjuring on my part. *Look!* You are here. But I can step right through you. It's as if you aren't there.

And don't give me heaven or transcendence or subatomic particles strewn across the universe or beyond—or any of that stardust. Or at least, don't give it by way of comfort before the fact. Don't make me contemplate an eternity of nothingness or indeed of bliss. There may be immense comforts in it, but they are immanent to the state. Teetering on the lip, there can only be dread and recoil. And you are not down there, or out there, or nowhere. There is no you. There only was. I am learning to live with that, but there will always be these lapses, these heart-lurching falls through trapdoors.

Resume.

But even these places unconnected to you seemed wrong somehow. I wanted to meet Josephine in a place to which I had no connection at all. So I booked a table at a restaurant new to me. It was recommended by a colleague. And that was a mistake too. The restaurant was fine. But I had introduced a clandestine note to the evening. Shades of assignation. We were somewhere we wouldn't be spotted. Though if we were spotted, so what? Yet another thing.

"You know why Jean suggested this?" Josephine asked. We had been seated at our table; water and wine had been ordered. "Because I am a widow and you a widower."

This coincidence of grief, Josephine explained, was the necessary first condition for her to be exposed to an evening of this sort. (She was immediately on eggshells here. Pointing something out; implying nothing by it. The teeth of my smile had something of the quality of glass or ice that might shatter if it had to keep up this surface brilliance for too long.) Friends were heedful on her behalf, Josephine continued, but a fellow initiate was assumed to be a relatively "safe bet." At the very least, there would be something to talk about at that difficult ice-breaking stage. (The stage at which we were, though I must say I was warming to this woman.) To take one example: one's new friend would be less taken aback if one were to run howling to the Ladies if some chance remark was to set one off.

This opener was funny and well-delivered. And I guessed that Josephine had trotted it out more than once. I knew from Jean that Josephine had been a widow for five years, so she had three years on me. At this stage, it was showing.

The wine arrived. I suggested she taste it as I had chosen the bottle at her behest. She nodded her assent to the wine waiter after the minimum amount of fuss, which I liked. We chatted about this and that. The starters arrived. We started on them.

Josephine's late husband, Stephen, had been in a wheel-chair, she explained. Not at the end, not as a result of his final illness or injury, but from the beginning, from before the time she met him and fell in love. This information she volunteered matter-of-factly, as if an able-bodied woman falling for a para-plegic man was nothing remarkable, which—to me at least—it still is.

To my shame—my added shame, perhaps—the next thought that came to my mind was how the sex was accom-plished. I recalled an incident during my student days when a friend observed of a couple he knew—the man was notably tall, six-six at least; the woman as notably short, no more than five-one—"Here comes team infeasible sex." How, my friend and I speculated, long into the evening, were organs and ori-fices aligned given this foot and a half difference. The conun-drum was a source of inordinate hilarity to us. Josephine and her late husband's feasibility issues were of a different order, of course, and more to the point—none of my business. But I was musing on them nonetheless and not paying much attention to what Josephine was saying, when she threw in that Stephen was latterly bedridden, which prompted—even more inoppor-tunely—mental images of her servicing in some way whatever needs he might still have had in that department in his latter-day state.

I pulled myself up. (*Servicing?* I know.) It was most inap-propriate to be thinking along such lines as Josephine, most movingly I realised now—now that I was listening to what she was telling me—spoke of her husband's painful last year. And yet, when I reflect on it, I do wonder if by bringing a bedrid-den Stephen to the table, as it were, Josephine wasn't banish-ing once and for all any prospect of bed and what might go with it. Not only the imminent prospect but the inherent one too. It had that effect on me, anyway. What I hadn't been anticipating I certainly wasn't now. Belt and braces, you might say.

It was perhaps rather hard on Stephen, however, for I now had an image of him which was firmly lodged in my mind. I couldn't shift it. Not even as Josephine went on to describe him in his prime, albeit wheelchair-bound, setting up and running a highly successful advertising company and finding time on the side to write a couple of plays, one of which I realised we had seen, at the Donmar or the Almeida or somewhere. *Greece, Lightning!*—remember? The title if nothing else, in my case.

Of course, Josephine had heard of you—and because of your work and not just your murder. She handled that as well as anyone, incidentally. Starting with a well-judged level of condolence; then avoiding the trap of suggesting your "legacy" must be some comfort to me. (It is and it isn't, but I don't like it to be assumed. She, I guess, must have Stephen's plays thrown at her as some crumbs.) Thereafter she left me the space to say what I wanted to say about your death (not much), and how I've been coping since (even less). That led me to share a few memories of our life together and indeed of your life and career independently of me. Only then did Josephine come back in with some standard, but obviously sincere, observations of her own about you and the impact of your work. She had had some mental health issues. (Doesn't everybody these days?) Depression, anxiety attacks. (Me too, I didn't add.) She didn't dwell on them. (Credit to her for that.)

At the end of this exchange, I observed, as now seemed to be required, that while we had both heard of the other's spouse, and they had doubtless heard of each other, the two of us were the unknown ones, the unsung partners.

We laughed cautiously at this thought. Neither of us wanted it in any way to imply destiny, a sense of a winding path leading to a fateful meeting. There was just a certain bond, that was all. The evening was turning out all right.

Then it took a turn for the worse.

First, Josephine expanded at some length on how Stephen's forceful personality, his dominant presence, and towards the end, his care needs, had been stifling for her, for all that she loved him very much. She had, she confessed, enjoyed a certain liberation in more recent years—the years after her initial, devastating grief had abated. A career as a model—given up shortly after marrying Stephen, when she had her first child—had been resumed with considerable success, there now being a "vogue" for "mature" women to model clothes that only women of their years, and only some of them, could afford. She named a few magazines she had appeared in, *Vogue* being one of them, and I did a reasonable job, I thought, of sounding fascinated, this being an aspect of life that I do not find remotely fascinating, in fact.

I didn't do well enough, though, for there was suddenly a distinct coolness in the air. She assumed a pouty expression (not unattractive; one could see how she would have looked as a young woman). She had talked about being a fashion model and I had assumed an air of superiority. I had come over all senior diplomat. She had expected better of me. None of this spoken, of course, just intuited by me from the smouldering sulk.

Then she asked me what I did and—touché, one might say—wheeled out her own impression of someone trying to look interested when it is clear they couldn't be less so. Worse, she insisted on making her own observations on the conflict, about which—to be brutal (it was getting to that stage)—she was woefully underinformed. I nodded along most uncomfortably, and I don't doubt some of my exasperation—though I hope not contempt—surfaced. The coolness had become a hard frost.

The mains had arrived and we were well through the first bottle of wine. (My doing, almost entirely.) I would have liked to have ordered another, but I didn't want to add a marked differential in the consumption of alcohol to the knot of complications that were making the evening such an ordeal. The result was that I faced, I calculated, a good hour with only half a glass of Merlot and the cold comfort of fizzy water to sustain me. I might just get away with a dessert wine, I thought. Though it was perhaps preferable if we skipped desserts. Then there was brandy with the coffees, if we didn't skip those too. Suddenly, the prospect of a solo nightcap back at the hotel assumed immense consolatory proportions. I would laugh about all this then, I thought, almost weeping as I did so.

But I have been skirting around the issue long enough. Yes, Josephine was a model. And yes, I suppose I did just casually drop that into the conversation as if it was neither here nor there, as if I am in the habit of having dinner with models. No big deal. No great shakes.

It wasn't like that, of course. This was my first time. And yes, I was struck, as anybody would be, by how very good-looking she was. Good-looking, I should add, in that way models tend to be, even "mature" ones. (All this spoken from the perspective of someone who is no expert in models, I might add—any false impression in this regard now having been removed, I trust.) Luminous skin, feline bone structure, good posture. She was pencil slim too, and her hair, even to my untrained eyes, looked as if it was well attended to. I pictured her at the hairdresser's every other day, which I guess counts as work in her line of business. But there was one thing about her hair that I found rather off-putting. It was long and lustrous, but old-lady grey. White, almost. I understand this is the fashion. But, as I say, I didn't care for the look.

What colour was your hair? Is there a colour called dirty blonde? It rings bells, yet they surely don't call it that on the label, and I know, in later years, your colour was coming out of a plastic bottle. Or being applied by your hairdresser. What was his name? Something almost comically apt, as I recall. Raimondo or something? This colour was your natural colour, the colour of your hair in youth, or young womanhood—when I first met you—which was a browny/blonde, just right for your unfussy, not-too-conscious-of-itself, mussed-up sort of beauty. Anyway, I'm sure I didn't say nearly enough how nice, how lovely, your hair looked in later years. You weren't a great one for those type of compliments, but even so.

Now, to answer your question—implied if not stated—no, I didn't "fancy" Josephine. A hideous word and concept. And it wasn't just the hair. She was obviously attractive, but I wasn't attracted *to* her. What I was, I will admit, was flattered. First, that Jean considered me in some sense a "match" for her obviously beautiful friend, and second, that Josephine appeared to feel the same. It wasn't that she had seen a photograph of me in advance or anything. (I sincerely hope not, anyway; I hadn't seen a photograph of her. At the risk of labouring the point, it wasn't to be that sort of evening.) Rather it was that she hadn't shown any sign on first seeing me—an undisguisable flinch, a just perceptible grimace—that she felt she had been set up with someone who wasn't in her "league" lookswise. And that was a boost to my ego, for if she was a "9," or at worst an "8," that made me (don't laugh) a solid "7," surely?

Oh, surely!

I make myself sound rather foolish, I realise; a vain old man totting up the points. Poring over leagues and matches. All I can say is that it is nice, once in a while, to be reminded that I am still attractive. Didn't you used to say I grew more attractive as I got older? Not to you, specifically, though of course . . . (Hole: stopping digging.) But generally. Generally? Friends had observed. Which friends? Never mind. Much laughter. One of those memories that hurt and heal at the same time. I am pleased to say some of the old twinkle is back. But bereavement takes its toll on all that: on one's looks, one's self-esteem, one's confidence.

There was of course that period. (Do I want to go there? Not really, but I feel I must be unsparingly honest.) There was this period, then—not in the first few weeks or months, but after that, in many ways the darkest period—when there was this sexual charge that surrounded me. This was nothing to do with me being an attractive older man that some of your friends might have quite fancied. It was nothing to do with me being an objective "7." It was electrical, chemical. It was wanton.

Your murder was a big part of it. This macabre celebrity of ours. You a celebrity in death; me a celebrity in grief. To some women, the combination of vulnerability and fortitude I showed in coping with your death bestowed aphrodisiac potencies. A weak man exploits that. Or falls victim to it. Much the same thing in the end.

It gets worse—some of them, I swear, wanted to sleep with you, as much as me. They wanted you to be in the bed with us—or, at least, to commune with you through me. Did I just imagine your name being shouted out? Probably. I was pretty out of it too. The whole business had a delusional, not to say delinquent, atmosphere about it. It was the most fucked-up fucking, which language tells its own story. Pick-ups, one-night stands—drunken invariably; groupies one might almost say. Preying on me at my most vulnerable, but it worked both ways. The sex was ravenous, animal, but not without tenderness and compassion. It doesn't make it any better—still worse, perhaps—but there were tears and hugs afterwards. Lonely people comforting each other as best they could.

But I won't pretend that I hated myself as a result. Well, I did and I didn't. I thought, how it would look? To you, yes, but also—God help me—to *the public*. Sordid, I thought, and so I felt a bit sordid. Disloyal, and so I felt a bit disloyal. But I also felt a sense of release. I needed it. Something—no need to go there—was pent-up, ready to explode. These women obliged. Was I doing something wrong? Maybe, but there were no consequences. I just walked away, night after night.

This is how and why men cheat, I thought. It is much more about the opportunity than the desire. For this short period, I had opportunities, I took them, I don't—let me say it again—regret it. Yet after a while I stopped. Though it would be more honest to say *it* stopped. There were offers still. But far fewer. Whatever had surrounded me—the charge, the aura, the miasma—had dispersed. I was having to work harder suddenly. Or rather, I would have had to, had I been minded to, which I was not suddenly. I was more my old self now. A sense of equilibrium had returned. Did I want to risk rejection and humiliation in order to sleep with this or that woman? I was appalled at my previous recklessness, if not the sex itself. That, in a way, it had helped. Though, I won't insult anyone's intelligence by suggesting it was a necessary part of the healing process.

For what remained of the dinner—we both passed on desserts but had coffees—I enjoyed being in the company of this attractive woman, of being *seen* with her, albeit by nobody I knew—which fact I now slightly regretted. I imagined these fellow diners thinking, perhaps even saying, "What an attractive older couple." And the notion that we were a couple didn't matter now, for only strangers looking on and seeing two people well-matched in looks but in nothing else could have leapt to such a conclusion. Nothing was going to come of this evening, that was settled once and for all. Josephine and I were not in any sense the other's "type." The whole enterprise, I realised, had been engineered by Jean because she was fully confident of that fact. The point of the evening was to allow me to feel precisely the sensation I was feeling now. We were easing into the home stretch. I had ordered that brandy and Josephine had joined me. Now that it was almost over there was no great rush.

As we were waiting for our coats, a strikingly beautiful young woman came into the lobby area.

She was on her own and took only a moment or two to locate the person she was looking for. Josephine. Her mother. It was not of course a chance running into. Josephine's daughter was the backup, the get-out—in the event that I *had* misread all the signals. "You're in town too, aren't you?" I could imagine Josephine saying on the phone. "So come along at, what, ten-thirty and say you thought we could share a cab home. Just in case." Josephine smiled a little sheepishly at being so transparent. I put out my hand and she took it. But she pretty much had to arch forward to kiss me on the cheek. She owed me that.

I should stop there. It is getting late. I am having that nightcap at the hotel bar. Another brandy. I know I shouldn't. There is just one thing I want to add before turning in. I have another long day tomorrow. There is a young woman, a waitress or maid, at the complex. I don't know why it is that I first noticed her. There are lots of staff like her, many of them young women, who work around us almost invisibly. Silently, certainly. This girl is not attractive. Or rather, she is only attractive because of her youth, which as we used to discuss is an attribute only valued by those who have lost it, are past it, who, however attractive they were in their own youth, are viewed by the young as old, and nothing more. Such are the indignities of life, I suppose, hers being the greater because she lacks the compensating sense of perspective: *all* she feels is unattractive. No boy her own age gives her a second glance, I'm sure. It is an observation I can make confidently, cruelly—despite never having seen her among boys her own age—as I remember being that age myself and I remember ignoring, confidently, cruelly, girls who looked like her.

And I was a shy, sensitive boy. It was always said of me. I had no great success with girls—the ones I did fancy—because of it. It was their mothers—and what was the use of that?—who took a shine to me. It wasn't until I met you that this changed. All through university, there was no one really. There was no sowing of wild oats with me. *You* were my wild oats as well as my . . . whatever comes next. *I dunno. Muesli? Rice Krispies? Coco Pops?* Please stop. I am getting the giggles. And I am trying to say something serious.

This girl never looks up, at me or at anyone else, as she wheels in the metal trolley and goes about replacing the mineral water and the bowls of fruit and the Turkish delight. She keeps her eyes down. It is painful to see. But she must sense that I am always looking at her, hoping—though also dreading—that I will catch her eye? I am still that shy, sensitive, cruel, confident boy. I would look away—or do I mean, blank her—if she was to look in my direction. I am afraid of her. Or do I mean I hate her?

The occasion that troubles me so much came after the most harrowing session of all of them. We had had described to us the injuries inflicted on female students during the occupation of the Women's University. There were photographs too. Broken bottles, pieces of wood, the barrels of firearms.

Of course, the young maid wasn't in the room for the session. But she came in soon afterwards to clear up. She and the older woman, who is about my own age. And perhaps because of the air in the room, some chilling reverberation, the girl was shaking. Or shivering. She looked even paler and more fragile than usual. Skinny, scrawny, rather red in the face, thin blonde hair, scraped back. As I say, nothing really attractive about her at all. But I couldn't stop looking at her.

There, I've told you. What were you expecting? Nothing

has happened. That would be preposterous. Yet what if those eyes, which never look in my direction, were to convey unmistakably that she wanted to? Wanted to, you know. Of course, they won't. And if they did, I would look away. To do otherwise would be a gross abuse of power. It would be inappropriate in every conceivable way. But it remains a recurring fantasy even now, even after the afternoon of the Women's University.

I will drop a note thanking Jean for the evening with Josephine at some point.

I had imagined—showing little imagination—a room in a house in Hampstead, high-ceilinged, book-lined, with busts and curios, heavy red curtains in front of double doors giving out on to a mature garden, a heavy red damask or brocade rug thrown over a low couch, piled with cushions. So little imagination, in fact, that what I am describing—you are doubtless ahead of me—is 20 Maresfield Gardens, the Freud Museum, Freud's last house, Freud's consulting room. Or a reconstruction of it.

We occasionally went to talks at the museum. Indeed, more than once you were one of the speakers. These talks were always fascinating, though I couldn't tell you the subjects of any of them now. Coming up in the next week or two—I have looked up "What's on" at the Freud Museum—is a talk called "On the Couch: A Repressed History of the Analytic Couch from Plato to Freud" (it is also the title of a book I have just bought it on Amazon), in which Nathan Kravis, "himself a practicing psychoanalyst," will tell how the couch became "an icon of self-knowledge and self-reflection as well as a site for pleasure, privacy, transgression, and healing."

It goes on: "Kravis deftly shows that, despite the ambivalence of today's psychoanalysts—some of whom regard it as 'infantilizing'—the couch continues to be the emblem of a narrative of self-discovery. Recumbent speech represents the affirmation in the presence of another of having a mind of one's own."

Though surely not. That is to say, I didn't really think "seeing someone"—as my GP deftly put it—would be full-on
Freud Museum, all-out analytic couch; I just didn't have much
else to go on that morning before I got there, that's all. That
and I was trying to distract myself, to think of something other
than this first session with a grief counsellor, which would be
starting in ten minutes or so, the taxi having dropped me off at
the Therapy Centre, a no-nonsense modern building, just off
the North Circular in Mill Hill. And it wasn't that I didn't
want to be there, that I didn't think it would be helpful, that
I didn't think I needed this counselling, it was that I *did*. Me,
the last person in the world anyone could imagine needing
such a thing. Even in these circumstances. And I include in the
incredulous, you, a great advocate of counselling, a practi-
tioner of it, though in a rather different field or branch of the
practice, I suppose.

That the experience was so strange and unfamiliar to me
was the first thing we talked about, in fact, in the light, bright
room, with its lime-green fabric tub chairs, and low table
with—I noted—a box of tissues placed upon it. And then that
this sense of unfamiliarity was itself strange given your profession. You had a consulting room yourself presumably? But the
fact was I couldn't remember ever having been to it. Or them.
Doubtless there were a number over the years in different
places. You moved around a lot. Nor could I remember you
ever having described any of these rooms to me. Or even saying when we were in Freud's reconstructed consulting room:
"It is nothing like my consulting room. Mine is . . . "—which
would have been an obvious thing for you to say there, would
it not?

A lot of what I said at that first appointment—and when I
said, "we talked," I should really have said "*I* talked"; that's
how it works, after all—revolved around my not remembering
things, or being unable to recall whether or not you had ever

said, or we had ever done, this or that or the other. It had been more than a year by then. Was part of it that I was losing my connection to you?

Perhaps. As I say, the counsellor, Caroline, was not to be drawn on this or any other question. Caroline, who I have largely consigned to the past, but who surfaces now and then. She was a bland-looking woman, of indeterminate middle age, but maybe that was a trick of the trade? I was the centre of attention, while she hovered, almost disappearing. Did I ever look her in the face? I certainly didn't ask her a single question about her own life.

It occurred to me—something had to; otherwise there would have been silence—that it would be rather intriguing to discuss losing you *with* you. In a professional capacity. What would you have done to help me?

Caroline said nothing.

That for one thing. *That* more than anything, perhaps?

Though I wanted to be there, *needed* to be, I couldn't help being—what is the phrase?—passive-aggressive. I think that is what I was being? Though was I best placed to judge? More your province. Not that I am expecting you to answer. This is not unusual in the circumstances, I assume? It takes a while for clients or patients or whatever you call them to lower their guard, to open up?

I had, I realised, not taken nearly enough trouble (and why was I suggesting it was any trouble?) to understand your work. Your *life's* work. That question again. Asked of you this time. What was it that you actually *did*?

Still nothing.

Here's a thing. The similarities with the role of a peace negotiator are striking. This thought must have occurred to me, to you, over all the years we were together, me conducting peace negotiations, you in a consulting room nothing like this one. We must have discussed it. At some point. While you were alive. Before you were dead. Murdered. Decapitated. We must have.

We didn't get a lot further that first time. We left it "there." You and I and Caroline. The fifty minutes had neither flown by nor dragged. In keeping with all that went before, I can't remember what I did after I left the session. It seems rather screenplay, but I think I just walked for hours and hours. In the rain. (No, that's too much.) Went to the pub, then. (Almost certainly.) Got drunk. (It follows.) Crashed out. A happy turn, though. Or as happy as it gets. I went back the next week. And the next. I "opened up," I suppose that's what you would call it.

It wasn't just the fact of your death, or the shocking nature of it, but all that followed which came flooding out.

For the aftermath was witnessed, and captured on mobile phones, by passers-by. The story went viral. Within an hour the death of Anna Dupont was headline news around the world. It was trending on social media.

What the footage showed was the attacker being wrestled to the ground by two other young Muslim men and detained by the police. The two men went on to appear at a vigil the following night with the 57-year-old husband of the murdered woman, a senior diplomat, highly regarded for his work on international peace negotiations. The vigil was attended by thousands of people and broadcast live. The husband called for calm, for people to come together, for reconciliation between communities. He said this is what his murdered wife would have wanted. He displayed great restraint and dignity. Or so it was said. He was much lauded. By Number 10, by Parliament, and in the media. Though he had little choice but to react this way. He could hardly weep hysterically and vow bloody revenge, could he?

He briefly became a celebrity. This is also the way of things these days. Ditto: that some good must come of it. So a foundation was set up in his wife's name that raised hundreds of thousands of pounds in its first week. Those hundreds of young women who write to me.

The story took a twist after a couple of days. The young, heavily bearded man, of "Middle Eastern" appearance, who everyone assumed was an Islamist, was identified as a member of a far-right British nationalist party. Not a convert to Islam, but a convert *from* it; a British citizen of mixed Algerian and English descent; Ali Hadj-Dixon had served in the British Army in Iraq and been radicalised by the experience—but in an unexpected way. The killing, which everyone had assumed to be random, now appeared to be targeted. Anna Dupont had recently been at the refugee camp in Calais as part of a delegation of distinguished doctors and lawyers. She had spoken out on the radio about conditions there and called on the British government to admit more of the asylum seekers and migrants into the UK. The far-right British nationalist party had denounced her in a video posted online, a video which featured a more lightly bearded, seemingly lighter-skinned "Corporal Ali Hadj-Dixon."

The widower of Anna Dupont and the two young Muslims attended another event, repeating the same messages of peace and reconciliation. Several mosques and Islamic centres had been attacked in the meantime. The family of the killer had been taken into police protection after threats from Muslim extremists. Public opinion was all over the place. No one knew who to blame. Everyone blamed each other. The story was out of control. #EndtheBlameGame was trending. And that was not the end of it.

Ali Hadj-Dixon was found to be suffering from a severe mental illness, brought on by post-traumatic stress disorder. The aftercare offered by the British Army to its soldiers who had served in Iraq was questioned and criticised. It turned out Anna Dupont had met her killer. She may have been helping him in some way, though not officially. He was not one of her patients. They had met in cafés near the research institute where she was based.

There were arrests of senior members of the far-right group. The home of the mother of one of the men arrested was firebombed. An extreme Muslim group claimed responsibility, though of course it was suggested by some that the far-right group had again carried out the attack and made it look like an Islamist action. No one was hurt, but the house was badly damaged.

The mother was interviewed and she denounced not the firebombers, but her son and the far-right group, saying they were to blame for the community tensions. They started all this, she said, for which she was widely praised on the left and denounced on the right. She was, it turned out, a veteran Labour councillor. With links to the far left. But the conspiracy theory pinning blame on the far-right group was later exposed as baseless. The firebombing *was* the work of an extreme Muslim group, previously unknown and promptly banned. The senior members of the far-right party who had been arrested were released without charge after a few days. The anti-terrorist squad said they were satisfied the killer acted alone. He was a lone wolf.

The husband of Anna Dupont gave an interview to the BBC—a longer one—in which he was asked how he felt about the killer. There was a social media storm directed at the interviewer who asked the question. "What sort of a question is that to a man whose wife has been murdered?" The widower's answer was this. Nothing. Or if anything, pity. To be honest, he didn't know what he felt. Confused, perhaps. He laughed as he said this. Live on air. This made some people feel uneasy. They said so on Twitter and Facebook.

"Laughing like that when his wife has been murdered like that."

A week later the killer hanged himself in his cell in a high-security police station.

There was an inquest, disciplinary hearings, an internal army investigation, a select committee inquiry. At the vigil to mark the first anniversary of the death of Anna Dupont, her husband was joined in his call for reconciliation by the veteran left-wing councillor whose house was firebombed, by her son who had been in the far-right party but had since left and was working for a counter-extremism unit at the Home Office, by a sister of Ali Hadj-Dixon, and by one of the two Muslim men who had wrestled Hadj-Dixon to the ground. But the other was absent, having been charged for his alleged involvement in a sexual grooming ring, though he was later to be found not guilty.

The story was a mess, quite frankly. Too many elements. So many twists and turns that it had become almost farcical. @Huffpost hastily withdrew its headline: THE NEWS STORY THAT KEEPS ON GIVING.

But on social media, #WhatNext? kept trending. Or the variant, #WTF?

But through it all the husband of Anna Dupont maintained the restraint and dignity that was expected of him. He "threw himself," as they say, into the work of the Anna Dupont Foundation, and as a result the reputation of Anna Dupont grew and grew.

Caroline didn't comment on the fact that I relayed all this in the third person. In fact—you've guessed it—she said nothing at all.

Just listened.

I completed the twelve-week course. It definitely helped. To some extent. Let me put it this way: I was in a better state at the end of it than I was when I started. I took a bunch of flowers with me for that last appointment. Caroline was most touched. Few clients were so thoughtful, she said—which struck me as unlikely.

"Of course, I *still* don't understand what it is you actually do?" I said. She laughed. And didn't say anything

Caroline. It is a while since I thought about her.

But I am telling you all this, why? The same reason that prompted the counselling: the thoughts.

As my GP said, and so did friends, these thoughts are entirely understandable, it would be strange if I didn't have them, and yet, look at me, look what they were doing to me, so I had to find a way . . . to . . .

What?

Not think them?

Well, not so obsessively. Put them to the back of my mind, so to speak. Look, they were destroying me. So I did that. Long story short, of course. Partly thanks to Caroline's counselling. Though what she actually *did*—this is getting repetitive—I couldn't tell you. Doubtless there were other factors. The passage of time: that old standby. Distractions above all. Following a ball or a hare. Pascal raged against it, but I must say I swear by my faculty to be amused by diversion. By which Pascal meant more or less anything other than contemplating "the eternal silence of these infinite spaces", of course. Though at least he had the grace to admit, God and salvation notwithstanding, that the prospect frightened him. The 78th *pensée* is a good one, by the way. *Descartes useless and uncertain.* No shilly-shallying there. Still, never trust a Pascal man over a Montaigne one, I always say. They wouldn't recognise themselves as such, but both sides at the talks are Pascalians *plus ultra.* And you see what has happened here? A step up from balls and hares, but diversion all the same.

Sometimes, however, the thoughts hurtle from the back of my mind to the front. They stop me in my tracks, so to speak. The trigger is God knows what? It isn't, as might be imagined, mention—or worse—of decapitation. Videos of beheadings have featured in our proceedings a number of times. I have watched them. I have forced myself to. And don't misunderstand me, but it is a good thing, a relief, that I have found myself having to. When my appointment as chair of the talks was first mooted, much was made of whether I could possibly be expected to sit through horrors so close to home. How could I maintain the necessary degree of emotional detachment? Most importantly, would the parties to the talks ever accept me as impartial? I don't want to be melodramatic, but I felt my career was on the line.

I argued strongly that what had happened to you had no bearing on my ability to do my job of thirty years plus. You had been a victim of terrorism, but, remember, Hadj-Dixon was not a jihadist. He was not an Islamic extremist. He was a British nationalist, a neo-Nazi. People often seem to forget that, which upsets me because he set out to sow just this confusion. This last point swayed it, I think. Anyway, I was appointed. I trust I have repaid the faith the governments showed in me. It was a risk, I suppose. Some eyebrows were raised in the media. And there have been occasional mutterings.

I had made myself watch videos before. Online. On the dark web, I think they call it. I may be wrong. This was no doubt an unhealthy thing to do; fixated and morbid. As ever, Caroline tried to give nothing away when I described how I had sought out these films, how I felt I had to see and in some sense experience what had happened to you: to immerse myself in the horror and gore. She tried, but I could see it in her eyes and in the moue on her lips: the obvious disgust and revulsion. An entirely natural reaction. I wasn't still watching these videos by this stage, I told her. A look of some relief. But stopping hadn't helped. Or rather, I still had the thoughts and in some ways the thoughts were worse.

Today they came, as they often do, in the early hours, a twist—those thoughts come too—on Larkin's "Aubade." The poem was a favourite of yours. "Most things may never happen: this one will." You were so afraid of death. You had been since you were a little girl, I remember you telling me. It was why you didn't like to be "caught without people or drink." Or work. I was awake, not at four, but not far off, and I was remembering all this, and that you could annoy people notably me—by repeatedly quoting lines from the poem—"That vast moth-eaten musical brocade"—and then, suddenly, I wasn't thinking about "Aubade," I was thinking about your decapitation.

Imagine being able to say these words? Sometimes I try to imagine it—and can't. Yes, my wife was beheaded. Yes, she had her head cut off. This is where the whole *swish, gone, pouf!* thing comes in: because it still doesn't seem real. Like something out of *The Arabian Nights* was how I put it—though, come to think of it, this is playing Hadj-Dixon's game too. Orientalism: that deadly trap.

What must it have felt like? ("Don't go there," a voice insists.) What did you know, sense, experience? ("Go there," comes the response.) I hate to think; I want to know. What?

Almost nothing, was what they told me at the hospital. Death would have been almost instantaneous. But even leaving aside those perfidious "almosts," this still leaves the instant. Light. Switch. Dark. If I can put it this way. In the instant of the switch there was something. In the instant you knew, you felt, you experienced *something.*

What?

Searing pain. Appalling realisation. Catastrophic shock. Some cocktail. These attempts to capture it don't come close, of course. Indeed, their function, it seems, is to distance me from the moment. From you. From whatever it was like, given that searing pain etc., etc. doesn't even begin to describe it.

At around this point, I generally find that I am dwelling on the sword. As you can imagine, it was much discussed at the time. (Just as I forced myself to watch videos, so I didn't spare myself the online chatter.) It was a broadsword or a longsword of some sort, or perhaps not, to summarise threads that went scrolling on forever and then some. (Did these people—in Kaohsiung and Belo Horizonte and Tampere—not realise I was watching and listening in? Did they perhaps get off on the remote possibility?) It was certainly very heavy, this sword. A policewoman tried to lift it and couldn't. (This was captured and put on Instagram and something like 100,000 people pointed out that the policewoman failed to follow the most basic crime-scene protocols. "She dropped a clanger," one wag observed.) And sometime later, this was widely reported, a forensics officer nearly severed a finger as he swabbed the blade for what exactly? Blood, flesh, bone, tissue, marrow. It was your neck all right. Your body was lying just there and your head right next to it. But apart. Which went to show that the sword was "lethally sharp," one reporter observed. Well, duh, another 100,000 or so people commented (or liked, loved, smiley- or sad-faced): it cut a woman's head clean off.

It was suggested, quite tenderly, such is the intimacy of social media, that you—and I—should almost be grateful for the super-sharpness of the blade. And likewise, for Hadj-Dixon's superhuman strength, agility, athleticism, balletic grace, hand–eye coordination, nerve, single-mindedness, ruthlessness. And his army training, when that became apparent. Few others could have wielded this immense sword with such force and accuracy as to cut off your head with a single swipe. In the hands of someone less superhuman, it could have all been horribly messy. Hideously gruesome. A sawing or hacking through flesh and muscle and windpipe and spine, as sometimes happens if the blade is blunt or the executioner inept. Not to mention other injuries—hands, arms being hacked off—as the victim tries to shield themself. As it was, the volume of blood was shocking. Witnesses reported seeing it pumping out of the neck of the victim. Great pools of it on the pavement. The mopping-up exercise was something to see, apparently.

So, thankful for small mercies, then. And smileyface to the people who acknowledged that this was all they were saying, others having pointed out their insensitivity, thereby virtue signalling insensitively. Give it a rest, will you. Why are you even RIPing Anna Dupont or sending her husband your thoughts and prayers? You don't know these people. They are complete strangers. Let them be.

Hello, I'm here! This—weirdly—is how I was coping.

Do you remember that trip to the Musées des Beaux-Arts? Of course, we went many times subsequently, but I am thinking of that first time. I remember you wanting to show me *Landscape with the Fall of Icarus* by Bruegel—or perhaps not; by Bruegel, I mean—though who cares. You were always impatient about these disputes over attribution. It was the poem by Auden that drew you to the picture and the gallery, which a friend of a friend pointed out that evening was actually called the Musées *royaux* des Beaux-Arts. "Yes, and not forgetting the *de Belgique*." Pedants, that was another thing.

Anyway, I remember us both sitting in front of David's *The Death of Marat*, which is in a nearby room to the *Icarus*. Where we discussed, inevitably, the legend of Charlotte Corday's execution by the guillotine. That look of indignation on her face after one of the executioner's assistants picked her severed head out of the basket and slapped it. Camus among many others had put the notion about. You were rather fond of the story. "Well, I should think she would be . . . "

Not true. This is why I am telling you all this: it is not true. That is to say scientists agree that a severed head does not remain conscious for anything up to several seconds after decapitation. Your head couldn't have looked up from the pavement at your neck spurting blood. You couldn't have had the thought—the one that appals the most—that your head had just been cut off. That your head—lying, how?: on its side, I presume, somewhat cockeyed—was now you, the conscious entity, devastatingly bereft. That in seconds you would be dead. The great dread.

So you—your head—couldn't have looked up and seen Hadj-Dixon, standing over you, wielding the bloody sword. "You! Oh, Ali!" Much speculation online on that front, as you can imagine. You taking it up the arse. Sucking his cock. Must have been. And then you chucked him, so he cut your head off. Bitch had it coming. These towelheads don't do women's lib. Respect for that at least.

"Please," Charlotte said gently, reaching forward to put her hand on top of mine. Others said it too. They also said—though Caroline (it is Caroline not Charlotte) didn't: "Please, Edvard, stop doing this to yourself. It doesn't help." Caroline didn't say it, because she could see it did. Help. The thoughts came and I had to go there. As deep down as I could stand. To the most agonising depths, until I could stand it no longer and had to surface. In this consulting room or wherever.

That was the only time, as far as I can recall, we—you and I, not Caroline and I—ever discussed decapitation. And here's the thing: I remember that afternoon very fondly. We discussed decapitation in the way two young people do when they are sitting together in front of David's *The Death of Marat*, never imagining that one day . . .

"You were how old at the time?"

I remember I looked up. Such a direct question.

"Our late twenties, I suppose. Anna had a friend working at the European Commission and we went over for a weekend. Strangely for a diplomat, even quite a young one, I had never been to Brussels before. We went on to Ghent, I remember. Though we had been to Ghent before."

There must have been something about the look on my face. Caroline smiled.

"You don't know Ghent?" I said. She didn't.

"We used to love Ghent."

This is what happens. Even without the expert navigation of Caroline, I am washed into gentler waters. I reached out for that box of tissues on the low table. This became a feature of the sessions. I took a moment.

We had once discussed Lockerbie, I said, picking up. For a moment, the name didn't register with Caroline. Then, yes, Lockerbie. Maybe we had watched a documentary about it. It wasn't at the time of the disaster. That happened one Christmas, or close to. We were in New Zealand that year, I remember: staying with friends in Auckland. Our discussion took place sometime afterwards, presumably on a significant anniversary. What we discussed was what it might be like to be on the Pan Am plane, just after it was blown apart, not—unfortunately, in the circumstances—having been killed by the blast, but still belted up in your seat, fully conscious, or coming in and out of consciousness, and hurtling towards the ground, with—how long?— a couple of minutes, perhaps?—to contemplate inevitable death.

"Well, it is hardly a contemplative experience, I would imagine." I can hear you saying that in exactly those words. God forgive us, that made us laugh. The whole conversation was, oddly, quite light-hearted and jokey. We went on to speculate as to whether two or three seats or a whole row might have fallen through the air together, intact. With all the occupants holding hands together. And singing. Singing "Always Look on the Bright Side of Life."

More seriously suddenly. Would you want to be with someone else at such a time? More specifically, would we have wanted to be together? A variation on the Phil and Babs question. We didn't say so, but I think both of us felt the same way: no. Better to face the end alone.

Understandably, I had lost Caroline by this point. Phil and Babs? More generally, she must have been thinking what a couple of crazies we two were. Though doubtless you get to see all sorts in your line of work. Crazies by definition.

I went on to explain the Phil and Babs story. She listened intently and made no judgement. And then I mentioned that I had been reading this book in which the author imagines being offered a different Faustian bargain. Either: have the years you had together and your wife dies young of cancer. (What had happened in reality.) Or: forgo those years (go back in time; you both take different paths in life) and your wife (now not your wife) lives into old age. The author chose, if I remember rightly, the first of these two, I need hardly add.

But what am I thinking? I have mixed things up somehow. The story of Phil and Babs had not come to me when I was seeing Caroline. Philemon and Baucis, yes, of course; but Phil and Babs, that was only the other day. And this other book? I am not sure about that either. I have read it and thought about it, but was that more recently too? It also makes me doubt whether I am right about Lockerbie. It makes me wonder how reliable any of the above has been.

I should mention that the thoughts this morning—now back in the present—have precipitated something of a crisis. If it can be called a crisis to find oneself sitting on a bench outside the National Gallery in Trafalgar Square at five in the morning. And I should qualify that "find myself," implying as it does that, as if by black magic, I had just appeared here—or that I cannot account for my movements or motives, either wholly or in part.

In fact, I can. I couldn't sleep. No change there. Then the thoughts came, as they can. And I needed, I felt, to get up, to get out, to *do* something to stop them going around and around in my head. A walk, I thought. Blow the hour! Blow the cold!

And if it was madness at all, it was a controlled sort of madness. *My* sort of madness, in other words. Not so mad, then, as to neglect to put a coat on over my pyjamas and to put on shoes, and indeed socks, the latter before the former. And, at the last minute, to tie a scarf around my neck and to remember gloves.

But still, I must have looked somewhat odd, as I exited the lifts at this early hour, fully dressed but not quite, and with no luggage. No nothing. No early flight or train to catch. No taxi booked. "Sir?" the night porter on the hotel desk enquired of me. Sleepwalking? If I was, there was—I thundered through—no stopping me. He left it. He sees a lot of nocturnal comings and goings, no doubt.

I was out of there anyway. Out on Northumberland Avenue. Then what? Well, I walked. A full five hundred yards. I can see the hotel I am staying in from where I am sitting. I got this far and thought, what am I doing? This is madness. So I sat down. On this bench in Trafalgar Square. Deriving from *Taraf al-Ghar* (Cape of the Cave) or from *Taraf al-Gharb* (Cape of the West). Who on earth told me that? In my coat, and shoes and socks, and pyjamas. Not much of a crisis, then, if crisis at all. I am in a city I know well, where I have lived off and on for many years, and in a part of the city I know well too. I must have walked across Trafalgar Square thousands of times. And I am just minutes from the warmth and luxury of my hotel. I have—I have checked—my key card with me. No wallet, no keys, no phone. But I can get back into my room without any fuss or bother. Yet for all that, I am struck by how alien the atmosphere is out here. Something about the hour, the light, the cold, the circumstances.

One thing that has surprised me is the large number of other people who are out and about at this hour. Though the fact that I am surprised only goes to show how pampered and privileged—and middle-aged—I have become. Clubbers and night owls are heading home or, for that matter, still going strong. The night is still young. For the still young.

And then there are all the early-shifters—the cleaners and porters and baristas. The shadows of the shadow economy. Looking shell-shocked and shattered, the tearing from sleep streaked across their blurred features. You hated early starts, those hideous jingly/jangly ringtones on smartphones positioned just out of reach of the outstretched arm.

Suffice to say, I am not attracting any attention amid all this human traffic. A duo of policemen, bulked out with holsters and pouches and cuffs and sprays and batons and tasers and torches and bodycams and phones and radios, walked towards me a few moments ago, looked at me, nodded and walked on. Perhaps they clocked my pyjama trousers, but so what? I think perhaps when I left the hotel, in some distress, I imagined I might end up in a police station or A & E or a secure unit.

That was the extent of my madness right there. Yet after this five-minute walk, if that, I sat down here. I am repeating myself. And I was as I am now. Calm, lucid, rational. Normal. As in, I feel like I generally do. In no sense do I feel out of control. Not now. Sometimes I have these dark thoughts about how my wife was killed and I lose it for a bit. But that's understandable, surely?

Entirely. Caroline is back. As a device. She exists, of course. I assume she does. I would have heard if she had died. Anyway, I haven't made her up. But now she is only in my head—remembered, falsely remembered, misrepresented, represented faithfully, summoned as and when. I rather think she would approve of my making use of her in this way.

A tramp approaches. Let me rephrase that: a homeless person approaches. He doesn't have matted hair and a ratty beard and a raddled face. He's not wearing a torn and soiled overcoat or pushing a shopping trolley filled with stuffed plastic bags containing God knows what. That "street look" went out with Thatcher. Indeed, perhaps he is not homeless at all. Though it is hardly likely that he is a night-time rambler, is it? And on closer inspection, the sensible clothes— weatherproof jacket, ski gloves, jeans and strong trainers; the sort of decent clobber dispensed at night shelters these days—are tired and worn and crumpled and grubby. He has probably come from the underpass into Charing Cross station. Stretching his legs before breakfast at St. Martin-in-the-Fields. Or come from further afield. Maybe he has been walking all night.

For a moment I imagine us sharing a cigarette or passing back and forth a can of something. He would have to have been the one to offer. I haven't either on me, of course. Just that key card. (One more check.) Indeed, it has been years since I've had a packet of cigarettes about my person (nice phrase, that). And for all that I drink too much, I haven't resorted to downing lagers or cider in the street. I don't believe I ever have. Perhaps as a student?

Why I imagined us—the homeless man and me—communing in this way I now can't imagine. (The moment has passed.) What bond is there between us? None. Unlike the policemen, this man didn't look in my direction or nod. He just walked past me. He is passing the Canadian High Commission now. Perhaps he is teetotal and doesn't smoke? Presumably some homeless people are? What prompted this, I now realise, is that I could murder a cigarette, not having smoked one for literally decades, or had cravings for one for nearly as long.

But the craving has passed. The crisis never was, I now feel. It would suit the moment if I could say that the first light of dawn was appearing in the sky. It isn't. It is still dark, still night. Larkin stretched the definition of aubade in naming the poem. Or rather, was being bitterly ironic in using it. They don't start serving breakfast until six, but I am already looking forward to my full English.

Can it really only be six hours since I was having dinner with Josephine?

My Suite

I loved our house. I loved that it was unremarkable, that we could have afforded somewhere bigger, grander, in a better part of the city. The care and indeed the money we lavished on the house were excusable because of its essential modesty. We were allowed to show it off, to be open, even gushing, about our love for it, in the way an owner can be over an old mongrel but not a pedigree dog, or a parent over a willing child, but not an obvious prodigy.

It sold the other day. And if that sounds impersonal, if it puts me in a passive place, absent from the action, then that is appropriate because I don't feel I had anything to do with it— the sale or the house. Both have been in the hands of other people for a while now. Various agents who have managed the house; various families who have rented it. I was neither sad nor happy about the sale. Just as I was neither sad nor happy about moving out of the house, handing the keys to that first agent, hearing that a young couple and their two small children were moving in. They had a little dog. Did I mind? Why would I?

Better friends understood. A house full of happy memories had become another happy memory, an encapsulating one, one that I will always carry with me, so to speak, in this "I-used to-love-our-house" way. Just as I will always carry the days and nights of wild-eyed roamings-around-the-house, when every single thing in it—not just paintings bought for special birthdays or treasured pieces from our travels, but potato peelers and handwash dispensers and napkin rings—connected us by a thread that seemed to offer the possibility of my reeling you back in, until the thread snapped, leaving me there in the dining room or wherever, with a candle snuffer or whatever, in my hands, empty-handed. Where was I?

In a different place. Free of that. Cut loose from reconnection. And on the day of my move, the house was just a shell. As I had a last look around, I wasn't thinking, "Goodbye, old friend." I was thinking, "Have I left anything behind?" I had cleared my mind of sentiment. Decluttered. Deep-cleaned. What I needed I had kept or stored. The rest? Gone. Sold, given to charity, junked. I remember thinking to myself—with a grim note of self-congratulation—that this must mean I was moving on emotionally. Moving and moving on. Not much of a play on words, but enough to lift my spirits for a moment. These were still difficult days.

What floored me was the new apartment. Another shell, but one I had to fill. Stuff I had—some old, some new—but how was I to occupy this space? I walked through the empty rooms—I got there an hour or so before the furniture delivery company—and despaired of the height, the light, the potential—all the things that in the abstract had sold me on the place. I wasn't up to the lifestyle it seemed to demand of me. I slept—and wept—that first night, curled up in a small corner of the big new bed, amid unopened crates and boxes.

The apartment is on the third floor of an elegant nineteenth-century building. It is high-ceilinged, with period features intact, and has massive doors, with massive locks that involve visible and audible—and most pleasing—movements of parts. I can imagine the satisfaction that comes from oiling these mechanisms. Tuning them almost, so that they sing in the sweetest harmony. No doubt a man can be found who has devoted his life to this task. A craftsman. A man to be envied.

The layout of rooms makes eminent sense somehow,

though I would be hard put to explain why. One just knows that the first room behind a door on the left as one enters the apartment will be the guest room and first on the right will be the kitchen—and that this is a most apt arrangement. The street-facing windows in the living room are almost floor-to-ceiling and give on to a balcony. It is an agreeable place to read, with a glass of wine—though (shades of Martin Frink and his balcony) I have only done so twice at most. Work takes me away a lot, of course.

I considered Stockholm, Oslo. But Geneva was most convenient, and it is a more interesting city than it is given credit for—not that whatever interest it has interests me much. London, I ruled out early. It was to do with this moving and moving on business, if you will forgive me bringing that up again. You are there: but that is the point. I kneel, lay flowers, but don't want to sleep beside your grave.

What about all our friends in London? I visit them often. I weekend away at least monthly, if not fortnightly. I am lucky; I get lots of invitations. On the home territory of others, I come into my own. I am rather a good house guest, I like to think. I help out, clear the table, stack the dishwasher, but know when I am not wanted in the kitchen. I give my hosts space, I take myself off to the living room, or the guest room, or to the summer house. If a walk or a visit to a gallery or pub is proposed, I am pleased to be of the party, but I don't mind being left behind either. I don't need to be constantly amused, talked to or sat with. I'm happy to be left with a glass of wine and a book. I never object to someone turning on the television. I put my book down. I stroke the cat or dog. I play with younger children. I chat to older children. I go to bed when it seems my hosts want me to go to bed. Early or late. I am good at reading the signals. I am no trouble. I am nice to have around the place.

I get reinvited anyway. "What are you doing for Christmas/New Year/Easter, Edvard?" I get booked up months in advance. I have to turn people down.

I don't invite people back to my apartment, though. It's not that I don't have room. The apartment is spacious. I have the guest room, a big double. It is very comfortable and is made-up as if for visitors. Fresh sheets on the bed. A clean towel laid out. A visitors' book. Why I bought it I can't imagine. I have leafed through it once or twice as if I may have somehow missed some visitors.

Then there is the cabin in Urke. We were always going to, if you remember? Get back in touch with my "Norwegian roots," that is. (Your exact phrase, with more than a touch of mockery about it, but my sentiment.) Not that I ever lived in the Vestlandet—just holidayed there as a boy, laying down a bank of memories that called me back—or so I always told myself.

Then last year a distant, much older cousin died and his widow, not wanting to keep the place, hardly having been there in recent years, got in touch. Would I be interested in buying it off her? There was no discount for being family. I paid a fortune for what is basically a shepherd's hut. (I could almost hear the old widow of the distant cousin cackling at the end of the line.) But what else am I going to do with our money? *Your* money, so much of it. Give it away, of course, a lot of it. To all the causes you supported. And then there is the Foundation. But no one, least of all you, would begrudge me this one indulgence.

Of course not, darling. Your Norwegian roots and all that.

With the cabin, I'm always telling friends to go up and stay—for as long as they like. No, of course I don't want them to pay rent. It is a way to pay them back for all their hospital-ity, their solicitude, their forbearance. And one or two have been up there. And invited me along with them—missing the point, I always say, laughing. When I go there myself, I want to be *by* myself. To get away. Not from them as such. Not individually, anyway. But collectively, perhaps. From being among them and yet always somehow apart. After a bereavement, being with other people—this is hardly an original observation, I realise—can be the loneliest experience of all. It is certainly when I feel the absence of you most keenly. Being single again, I have found, is harder than simply being alone. It still jars so.

Even assuming it was practical to do so, I would not want to set foot in our old house—so loved—ever again. It is, as they say—another grim note—of satisfaction this time—dead to me.

I looked in on the Geneva apartment—*my* apartment—during this whistle-stop. "Looked in" is right: it captures that sense of visiting a distant elderly relative for the briefest time possible out of a sense of obligation. The flat exudes a sullen air when I first let myself in—unvisited in ages, it is grudging in its welcome. "Oh you . . . " as it were. Although it is still winter, and this big freeze has followed me down from the mountain and around the continent, I threw open the windows on the pinched resentment of the apartment. Blew some cold air up its dowdy skirts, so to speak.

I note that I am gendering the apartment as a grumpy old woman—which won't do these days. *Or any days.* And we exaggerate for effect—me and the apartment. Two grumpy old men, then, with a harrumphing regard for one another, though no love lost.

In fact, it—*he*—gets a regular visitor—a bright and breezy young woman who comes in and cleans and freshens once a week. Only once have I been there at the same time as the cleaner. She called out cautiously from beyond the front door when she realised that the apartment was not on its own. I was making coffee in the kitchen and did quite a good job of seeming to welcome this intrusion. "*Bonjour. Entrez. Je suis le propriétaire. Oui, M. Behrends. Bien qu' Edvard, s'il vous plaît. Ravi de vous rencontrer . . . Monique, c'est vrai. Non, ne me dérange pas."* She—Monique—cleaned with a diligent cursoriness. (Necessarily, the actual amount of cleaning that can be done is limited, but she stuck at it for the full two hours.) She was constantly around me and behind me, singing gently to herself, singing along to songs in the buds in her ears, as I endeavoured to get ahead of her, moving from room to room, unable to settle. I had a flight booked for later that afternoon. I wished I had booked for the earlier one.

My presence—the fact of me, in the apartment—must have intrigued her somewhat, I fancy. The mystery owner. "He does exist!" To people like her—living and working in the same city every day, rarely, if ever, leaving a narrow circle of family and friends—my peripatetic life—London one day, Paris the next—only occasionally, and then only fleetingly, visiting the apartment that is nominally my home, must seem alien. To be envied, perhaps? To an extent. But pitied too. Every sterile surface and unused utensil reflected back on me. What sort of a life was this?

A Monday, I think it is. Her day for cleaning. I leave things like her days to my managing agent, a young woman I have never met. All by email. Yesterday was a Thursday. I hadn't been to the apartment for a couple of months. My managing agent is supposed to deal with it, but some post had accumulated in my pigeonhole downstairs in the lobby. A neighbour—a designation I bestow only because he clearly lives in the building; I don't know the man—nodded to me as I retrieved my letters. (There was a stray birthday card. From Dom and Lindy.) He was carrying an ornamental dog rather as one might a baguette, though presumably this snooty, snouted creature (I took against it straight away for some reason) would deign to walk at some point. We are not far from the Parc de la Grange. Nor from the Quai Gustave-Ador. He—the dog, that is—was wearing a tartan waistcoat. His owner was wearing a green loden coat, as would appear to be mandatory among Swiss men of his age.

He was also wearing snow boots. I was in business coat, suit and formal shoes, the same outfit that had been inadequate for the weather in Berlin, London, Paris, and now here. My neighbour had just come down in the lift. He had hauled open the brass concertina curtain with a clatter. I was going up the way he had come down. Why am I telling you all this?

It is not that the apartment is not done out most comfortably. Our decades-long accumulation of books is there. As is most of our less extensive art collection, with some additions I think you would approve of. (I have had some pleasant afternoons at art fairs in recent months.) So too is what furniture and others of our possessions that were transferable and suited this very different space. Yet for all that, there is nothing really of our house in the apartment. I have adopted the studiedly neutral mode of living of a leading diplomat, of whom there are hundreds, living just like this, across Geneva. And in cities like Vienna and New York. What is lost is all the funkiness and edge you brought to the party. That had to go, I felt. I couldn't replicate it. I didn't have the heart for it without you.

I find myself—today and on other days—wandering about this space I have bought and furnished, and which I pay to be kept ready for me, as one might a museum once the house of a rich merchant of some sort. A man of taste but at the same time rather dull. There are areas which might as well be roped off or behind glass. *Please keep off. Strictly private.* Can I ever imagine having a dinner party—or even dinner on my own— at that dining table, for instance?

This sense of disconnection has its compensations, though. Climbing into bed in the master bedroom, slipping between the sheets, immaculately laundered, ice-cold but sensuous, is deliciously transgressive. A volunteer guide will find me here in the morning and tut-tut-tut and turf me out. The girl who cleans will come in and see this minimal disturbance—on one side only of the bed, of course—and try to imagine the night spent. (I concede there is something rather creepy about this imagining of her imagining.) In the same way, leaving a single teabag in the biodegradable waste bin—this one tiny thing to bag up and dispose of—gives me a kick somehow. Otherwise, what am I doing here? At the risk of repeating myself, I seem just to be looking around. Aimlessly traipsing. A half-day in a foreign city before catching a flight.

I dined, as I tend to do when I am here and when not required to dine elsewhere, in the brasserie around the corner. It is the type of restaurant that gets described (it would have been by you) as "just a little local place that we rather like"— which is to undersell the food, the service, the general ambience, but with good reason. Nobody—and the owners and staff can be included—wants it to become more than it is. It doesn't need to attract a new clientele, or to bring in tourists. It has worked out the magic formula. It is always full, but they can always find you a table. There is no need to book. Everyone is a regular. "*Ah, Monsieur . . .*"

Almost invariably I dine alone. In that now familiar "happy to be sad to be alone" way of mine. As the evening wears on, I lean and swerve into the table, the book that is open in front of me swimming in and away from me, pleasingly. I find at the end of the evening, or the following morning, that I have read only a page or two at most. And forgotten that page or two almost completely. I am competent, though, through great concentration and precision guidance, to order the final one-too-many drink without slurring—perhaps a Calvados or Benedictine— and then to settle up, retrieve coat and bag and umbrella, and take the short walk back to my building. There is perhaps some weaving along the way—and some evidence of that when fresh snow has just fallen. The hush in this quiet neighbourhood on snowy nights is immense. The odd car shushes by all but silently and seemingly quite without occupants. The apartment blocks are shuttered up. One could run down the middle of the street, kicking up powder, laughing and shouting, and the sound would echo around the city, the lake, the mountains—and away. No lights would appear at windows.

At the front door to my building, and then again at the door to my apartment, the key describes airy figures of eight until through some magnetic attraction it docks with the lock and magics me in. Back in my flat, I am sobered for a moment by its utterly cool unrelation to me. Let me just crash here tonight, I think, and tomorrow I will be gone.

Before bed, I attend to the necessary ablutions in my pristine, white-tiled bathroom. These ablutions are strung out like a dream. Ten minutes feeling like an hour. Hangovers I treat prophylactically—which may extend a certain brain death into the indefinite future, I don't know.

The following morning—this morning—my head in an ibuprofen-induced neutral, I pack the suitcase I never really unpacked and leave the apartment with as little sentimental parting as I would a hotel room. If I could I would hand in the key. But there is no concierge here.

Six hours later I am back. Yes, I am in this hotel room: the suite—bedroom, sitting room, bathroom, and balcony—that has been a home of sorts these last few months. It has served me well. I am back on the mountain and it is good to be back. I go out on to the balcony, hail the view and breathe deep.

The cleaners here have cleared away what disorder I left behind (not much). They have tidied my things (clothes) into wardrobes and drawers; piled them (books and papers) up neatly on tables. (Again, not much.) But for as long as it lasts, as little as it is, I am happy to call this my own. The bar beckons and I will greet some familiar faces.

Peace talks.

M y initial reaction on learning the news—some sort of defence mechanism?—was to make up silly puns in my head. "Noor is no more." Or "Oh, *Noor*" (requires Geordie accent like that character, Ruth, in *The Archers*. Yes, I still listen to it: your favourite radio programme).

The news was, though it was in no sense broadcast, that Noor had been "recalled." I learnt this only after noticing that he was absent from the morning's, then the afternoon's, proceedings. That is unusual in plenary and so I enquired.

As Noor is—was?—only the Number Three, my team didn't feel it needed to be flagged. This was reasonable enough. What wasn't reasonable, what unnerved me and would certainly have unnerved my team, was that I was so shaken by the news. For that very reason I trust I betrayed nothing of my feelings. I am practised enough at the inscrutable, the deadpan, to have got away with it, I think.

Let me not exaggerate the extent of my concern. I was somewhat thrown by the news, that is all. "Recalled" can mean to certain death, or immediate imprisonment, or summary dismissal. Or at least has done, in my experience. But it can mean other things. It can mean for consultations or instructions. Noor might very well return. I have known that to happen. Perhaps the whole thing will turn out to be an elaborate piece of theatre. As it is, they are constantly trying to rush bits of paper into proceedings. Envoys arrive, "hot foot" as they say, like bit players in Shakespeare, with supposed concessions or new proposals or evidence that must be heard.

Sabbagh knows, presumably. Why Noor has been recalled, that is. But Sabbagh is never going to tell me and I am never going to ask him. If Noor returns, he returns. Otherwise he is history. The waters have closed over his head. We move on.

I thought all this and yet I also thought: is it somehow connected? Am I somehow responsible? Connected how? Responsible in what way? Having met Noor that once in the churchyard and exchanged a few words? Because I accepted— or at least didn't return—the gift of the Koran? Well? Well, what? Who is interrogating who here? My conflicted self, it would seem. I came to no conclusion.

That I am distracted, that I have had difficulty focusing on proceedings, has had no bearing on the talks, I might add. They are going well. Around and about me, as it were. With me not fully or at all engaged. (I have raised my gavel once or twice, thought better of it and put it down again.) I should add too that the talks progressed—notably so—during the few days I was away, visiting capitals, my deputy in the chair. This idea that I am orchestrating the talks, that without me they would stall or fall apart, is more than ever an empty boast. Am I even a calming presence, a still centre around which progress swirls? Am I not just sitting here, in the middle of it, neither here nor there?

This question again of what do I actually *do*? Such is the progress towards a settlement that it increasingly looks like the main thing this time will be to take credit where it isn't due—the one comfort being that, when I report up, to governments, ministers, prime ministers and presidents, the credit will spiral up and away from me too. A Sherpa, even the most senior of them, does not get to plant the flag at the summit. That is one of our little sayings and I have always taken comfort in it.

I played a familiar card. I called an adjournment—not on the first day back, but on the second morning. (There was no sign of Noor, I need hardly add. I was not thinking of Noor any more. Will I ever?) There was surprise, one might almost say consternation, in the room. I didn't need to explain my decision to anyone else and I didn't. The explanation I offered to myself was that I felt we were in need of a pause—a timeout, as the Americans call it. Others might ask: why risk losing momentum? Why not power on? Had I said anything, I would have said that I thought we were perhaps running away with ourselves, hurtling too fast towards the finish.

I know some will speculate that I don't want this to end. That this is all I have in my life now. But I repudiate that. These talks are not some sort of emotional crutch without which I would crumple. I want a deal as much as the next man—and like him (this is still a man's world, get over it) I want it as quickly as possible. Indeed, I want it more, I'm sure. There are others who would spin things out for fear of what will come after. Not me. I will move on to the next round of talks. It isn't as if there isn't a waiting list of conflicts and crises in need of mediation. *My* mediation. My special skills. Whatever they are, whatever it is that I am good at, which must be something, as I have enjoyed a long and distinguished career pursuing it.

No, the fact was—let me repeat—that I felt things were getting a bit overexcited; there was—that strange potency in the room which happens sometimes—too *much* give and take, too *much* understanding and conciliation. It happens sometimes when a group of people, even mortal enemies, are locked up away from the world, particularly up here, where the air is so thin and hysterical, a sort of laughing gas. Everyone gets just a bit carried away.

For the first time ever, I have come out on the walk—the group walk—by myself, in the middle of the day. The snowfield, the icy bridge, the stand of trees, the steep and rocky climb—the peaks, the peaks, the peaks . . .

I am going to miss this, I will admit. To be up here and to be working—far from it all, but at the centre too.

It is positively hot. The snow has melted away completely in some places. Green patches. Water dripping from the trees.

I will go down—I must. My team, the two delegations, are waiting. They are locked away. There is danger inside these locked rooms. Positions can harden again. In the absence of the other, suspicion of the other inculcates and festers. I need to get down from this high place, my dizzying elevation, to race back. Who am I that I would threaten all this?

I feel very small. I will make myself even smaller. A minuscule man. A homunculus with a gavel. Laughable, puffed up. But we must bear with him. What he offers is humility and service. Let's get this done.

There was no ceremony as such. That will take place some weeks from now with the political leaders taking centre stage. The stage will be set with flags and flowers. The flags of the parties to the settlement; the flowers in the colours of the flags and otherwise white to symbolise peace. A small audience, consisting of the staff of the political leaders, members of the negotiating teams and various other dignitaries and diplomats, will be ushered into the hall. There will be a media pen for the larger number of cameramen, photographers and journalists. The whole event will be taken live on CNN, BBC World, Al Jazeera, RT, and the rest.

The leaders will walk to a desk at the front of the stage and sit down at their designated places. They will each have a water glass and a choice of bottles of mineral water. A plump leather folder will be laid on the desk before the leaders and they will sign on the line indicated to them, using plump fountain pens. (What happens to these pens afterwards? I wonder. Montblancs, every one. Who pockets them? And where does the leather folder with the signed treaty inside end up? I ought to know, perhaps. The flowers, I gather, go to local hospitals.) There will be handshakes, smiles and applause. Cue a lightning storm, with hail thrown in, of shutter and flash. I will be on the far right of the picture as you look at it, though you won't be able to see me because I will have been cropped out before publication. Take it from me, then, that I will be smiling and applauding too. Until someone shouts, "Cut"—not literally—and we disperse.

I have explained before that a peace deal is a victory of sorts. But one is reminded also of the scorn directed—rightly, I generally feel—at educationalists and child psychologists who disapprove of competitive school sports. Where there are no winners, or everyone is a winner, all you are left with is a bunch of losers, right? Away from the cameras and the journalists, there will be no sense of elation or even relief. We have come down from the mountain on to the plain. The prospect is a bleak one.

Consider the nature of the deal we have just concluded. A country divided in a highly artificial and unstable way. Lines drawn, zones designated, corridors created. All of this work with pencils, rubbers, rulers, and set squares (again, not literally: it is just how I imagine it—shades of colonial-era map-making and border drawing). And all of this overseen on the ground by a UN "observer force"—which is to say, a military force denied the power to act militarily. Factions within both sides to the deal oppose it bitterly—as they did the process which brought it about. They will be looking for every opportunity to destabilise and destroy. They will *have* every opportunity.

Peace may have been declared, but tens of thousands of people are dead, as many again have been injured, and many hundreds of thousands are internally displaced or living in neighbouring countries as refugees. Whatever the outcome of the war, the majority of these people would have sacrificed lives, limbs, family, friends, and homes in vain. Whatever the outcome of the war, most people would not have gained in any personal way from the years of fighting. Under the terms of the peace deal, the number for which this is true rises to precisely zero. The two sides have fought hard, and negotiated hard, to get back to the status quo ante (yes, that again)—except worse.

Their ethnic and religious differences have not been resolved, nor have any of their political and economic grievances. Indeed, these divisions and enmities have deepened and indurated. On top of which, whole districts of their main cities have been razed, important industries like tourism and agriculture have been devastated, infrastructure and the utilities destroyed.

Aid will flood in, of course, and reconstruction projects will start up, but primarily—or so it will prove—so that corruption and fraud can once again flourish. Electricity and the water supply will be unreliable and intermittent at best. Unemployment and poverty will remain endemic. An interim power-sharing government will be set up to pave the way to "free elections" and "democratic rule," but politics will be characterised by suspicion and recrimination. The old tyrants will still dominate; the old ways of doing things will persist. Assassinations and bombings will occur daily.

And remember, the imperative that brought the parties to the negotiating table was exhaustion from years of fighting— years of fighting with no prospect of victory or indeed defeat. It was not the prospect of peace. Not even the peace-makers within the parties—more precisely, the *warring* parties: they were forged for war—wanted peace for its own sake. What they wanted—or rather, needed—was a pause, a breather. A chance to recuperate and regroup.

(What, I find myself wondering, is the translation or equivalent in Arabic for "a breather"? Is it the sort of word that Noor would use? I doubt it somehow. Which is a pity. Nice expression "a breather": a "good man" turn of phrase. Yes, Noor sometimes comes to mind. Not frequently. No more frequently than the rest of them—and I include my team. We have all gone our separate ways, never—in many cases—to meet again. Just think how many people pass through one's life—not literal passers-by, not people opposite one on a train

or next to one on a plane, but people one has worked with for
a time or attended a conference alongside or interacted with in
some reasonably significant way—who one will never meet
again; the many, many thousands—who are, in effect, dead to
one. Alive still, most of them; actually dead, some of them.
But what is the difference? It is the promiscuity of acquain-
tance in the modern age that leads to this casual annihilation
of lives beyond one's own. It ought to prepare one, inure one.
It doesn't, of course.)

But I have got ahead of myself. This was the moment of triumph. The peace-makers had made a peace. And yes, as I have
been known to joke, "You are never going to be out of work if
your business is making peace." Or to put it another way—
another of my jokes, "Nirvana is not around the corner." But
this was not the moment for sardonic wit, for black humour. It
was—we must try to bask in it—a moment of light.

Though of light comedy most of all. Think of it this way:
such an occasion gives rise to certain social niceties that, with
all that has gone before, are not easy to pull off but are the
more endearing for it. So, there was one final rap of my gavel
to ragged cheers and then we were all on our feet suddenly.
And there was mingling of sorts across various lines. Uneasy
mingling—but mingling all the same. Certainly, some shaking
of hands; less certainly, some slapping of backs. But at the same
time, we didn't quite know where to put ourselves or quite
what to say.

As I say, no ceremony and no standing on ceremony. Rather,
a ramshackle democracy broke out. Girls—and boys—from
the simultaneous translation booths spilling down on to the
floor of the conference hall to join us. The delegations break-
ing ranks, if briefly, if tentatively. I was among the mill and
throng, feeling none too comfortable. Unmoored from my
established position. Deprived of my elevated status. I was
reminded of the odd occasion on which I have attended a

church service and the minister has invited the congregation to share the peace. "Peace be with you." "And also with you."

"Congratulations, Ambassador Sabbagh."

"Congratulations to you too, Mr. Behrends."

A team photo, someone said. We were all one team suddenly. How about that! Not for the official record, it was stressed, but for showing to family, for a keepsake. Where to stand for this picture was a matter of great—greatly forced—amusement and awkwardness. Short ones at the front, tall ones at the back. Hands were put on shoulders to manoeuvre people into position. There was gentle jostling. Some fixed grins. "Come on, Dr. Faroud, no one can see you lurking there!" The delegations would not be split up or mixed together, however. One on one side of the line-up; the other on the other. An incorrigible stiffness reasserted itself, for all that the young people in the negotiating team and in SimulTrans were determined to maintain high spirits.

"What is cheese in Arabic?"

"Cheese?"

"Yes, we say 'cheese' for photographs."

"Cheese in Arabic, my friend, is *jaban*."

"Altogether now: *JABAN*."

There was no question of alcohol, of course, but a few bottles of something sparkling were produced—the girl with the metal trolley appearing and then disappearing, head down, terrified. The extended exertion of easing the corks from the bottles elicited more forced laughter. At last! Sugary fizz was frothed into plastic cups. There was no clinking, but rather a squashy pressing together. The delegations started to gather up their folders and files. To snap shut laptops and power down screens. Just think of all the ghosts in those machines. There was now a distinct feeling of unease that there had been this outburst of informality—almost of levity.

I was sent a stern note, first by one side and then the other, that under no circumstances were any of the photographs to be posted on websites or social media. All staff were informed. The idea of that team photograph with us all—or at least some of us—shouting "*JABAN*" was both funny and terrifying. Imagine that doing the rounds? Talk about a diplomatic incident.

The work on the official communiqué had begun. I had started a ring-round of capitals. The delegations had withdrawn to their floors. To pray. To implore harsh judgements on enemies and infidels. And to seek blessing on their own peacemaking. Allah being pulled both ways yet again.

Still, we had a deal. As is the way of it, we didn't—and there was seemingly no prospect of one—and then there was—and we did. What happened so suddenly to resolve the intractable business of prisoner-of-war swaps? Or the question of war graves? Or the flying of flags on public buildings? Or parity of access to the one deep-water port? Sheer exhaustion played a part. Sheer grinding tedium too.

One after another and headlong, the Working Groups reported back that they had reached provisional agreements on the various points of contention. Schedules and Texts found itself scrambling. I called in the *chefs de mission* who sat next to each other in easy chairs for the first time. I had tea brought in and baklava. A nice touch, that. "Are we concluded?" We were and within the hour we were in a final plenary to slot the pieces together—and slot they did. Like blocks of finely sanded and well-oiled wood. *Parquet*, I remember saying to myself in an almost ooh-la-la accent. Call it high spirits. I was giddy with it for a second or two.

Closing statements could have undone all the good work, sliced open and reinfected the sutured wounds. But they were got through. Like that last half-mile of a marathon. Do you remember my one and only? A bandy-legged Mr. Bean treading water up the Mall, was how you described it. I think it was you. Then they draped a big golden Crunchie wrapper around my shoulders. My time: just over four hours and thirteen minutes. We went for tea in the Ritz, I remember.

As the closing statements wound on, I began to ponder whether it was actually possible to prop eyelids open with matchsticks. I tried to imagine the coarse surface of the match heads scratching my corneas; the wooden ends wedged in the bone shelves of my eye sockets. Holding it all together, unblinking, until . . . ping! What was everyone else thinking? What nonsense was not diverting them? Molten exasperation churned inside me suddenly. Intolerable fidgetiness took hold and generated heat. Intolerable heat.

Either side of me the doodles of deputies spiralled in on themselves, becoming blacker and blacker, more manically self-absorbed, until they broke the skin of the paper of notebooks, or started injecting black blooms of dye into the spongy veins of the ornamental blotters. These blotters had black leather frames with the crest of the hotel group inscribed in gold. The most extraordinary detailed work to produce something I hadn't until now—or only tangentially—noticed. Like the work that medieval stonemasons lavished on gargoyles high up in the great cathedrals. Chartres, Bourges, Reims . . .

And yet, these closing statements served their purposes. Monumental sanctimony and self-righteousness were strutted. A breathtaking carve-up of credit and blame. One last round of grievance and recrimination. But that was fine; these were exercises in going through the motions. The poison had been drained. There was open yawning and the drumming of fingers as the other side awaited their turn. All that remained for me et cetera, et cetera.

After the first sip, the fizzy drink was largely left untouched. It had a nasty, diesel taste, it turned out. Once the delegations had left us—and after a respectful pause—I suggested we might retire to the bar. I didn't say it, but it was clearly implied, "for a proper drink." Some of the team came, some didn't. The party, to the extent it could be so described, broke up after a round or two. People were already looking forward to getting home, to seeing loved ones. I didn't feel sorry for myself. I had another couple of drinks. Ordered a burger and fries. It would have been nice to phone you, as I did in the past, but there you are.

I should say at this point that I am not on my balcony, or in my suite, or in one of the bars or cafés of the resort, or in the *Gaststube*. I am not in the mountains at all. I have left them for good. Packed up and gone. A month has passed. The official signing of the peace deal will take place in a fortnight. No difficulties have arisen, but negotiations over scheduling, the precise choreography and stage management of the ceremony, take time. These I have left to able deputies, who are working with junior representatives of both parties to the deal. The caravan has moved to Vienna, the agreed site for the signing ceremony.

Where am I, then? As far from any of the above as it is possible to be. The West Indies. On a short break. On my own, of course. No change there. Perhaps there will be more evenings out with other Josephines? *In due course?* Quite so. But these will be very occasional variations on the main theme. The success of the evening out with Josephine has convinced me of that. My first-order relationship from now on will be with myself alone. I contemplate this fate with almost complete equanimity. I am getting used to this solitude of mine; dare I say it, even getting to *like* it.

Here I am, then, in this Caribbean resort complex, in my apartment, on its dark wood deck, which sits on tree-trunk struts, projecting out over a rocky, tropical garden that tumbles down a mountainside towards the sea. The apartments have been placed—doubtless with great care; this is, of course, an "eco" resort—in a forest of tamarind and coconut and cinnamon and turpentine and calabash and palm—such names to conjure with; a forest of exotics which covers not just this mountainside, but the mountain range behind the resort and the headlands that half encircle the bay.

There is a hammock, but I can't be doing with that. Remember that one time? It wasn't so much getting in as getting out. I am in one of the two easy chairs. Much safer. A pile of books beside me on a low table—and a long drink. A rum punch. And not my first. Bear that in mind. It is hot but without being stiflingly so. There is a sea breeze. I have had a snooze; I will be going for a swim. Then it will be "happy hour" in the clifftop bar.

The horizon line—a solid colour block of sea blue aligned precisely with another of sky blue—is—according to Pythagorean Theorem (I have looked it up)—some ten or twelve miles distant from the eye. Yet beyond it lies not shipping lanes or the Venezuelan coast or more sea that I cannot see because of the infinitely subtle curvature of the planet. None of that. What lies beyond as I look out on it now is . . . as good as it gets. An intimation of the Ultimate, if you will. Or at least, the opportunity with some tranquillity of the mind—and the minimum of self-consciousness—to contemplate it. Though self-consciousness is doing what it does here, you'll note, by dint of my referencing its near absence. This is the trouble with being in the quotation-marked or italicised now, I find. "Now," you think, and it's gone. *Now*, you think again, and it's gone again. Of course, one *is* in it, but in saying that, one isn't. Schrödinger's cat comes into the equation, if I'm not mistaken. Which I very well might be. Anyway, before you know it, one is playing a game—or the cat is: picture its paw poised to strike—of Whack-A-Mole with now.

The philosophers and theologians, the gurus and mindfulness coaches, have been over this ground endlessly, I realise. The eternal and unattainable now. I tried mindfulness, by the way. And meditation, the same thing before the rebrand. In fact, they were both *prescribed*. By Caroline. I got them free on the NHS. (This was after the grief counselling.) And I am always returning to the philosophers and—to a lesser extent— the theologians. The problem, as ever, is concentration. I might pick up Cioran's *Tears and Saints*—it is what I have beside me; it's not especially apropos—only to put it down again moments later, some thought having occurred.

Back to the horizon. For a moment. Concentrate on that. I *know*, but we're with the ancients on this one, aren't we? Perhaps the mythological quality of the transatlantic flight has something to do with it. The Icarian colours and textures and moods. The flying through time and the weather. The chasing the sun. For exactly this.

At the very least, what's out there, beyond the vanishing point, is some sort of transcendental catch pool, with an Escherian system of aqueducts circulating all this overspill of the mind. And I realise, of course, that all I am saying here is that the natural wonder which an infinity pool was designed to mimic looks . . . like an infinity pool. But then, there might be a certain profundity in the redundancy.

There is one of those here, inevitably: an infinity pool. One can swim up to the edge of it and look out on the real thing. With—if one cared to; the barman could surely fix it—a blue curaçao cocktail lapping right up to the rim of one's plastic cocktail glass. For the Montaigne of mind, the connoisseur of pleasure in the moment, this is full-package-good-as-it-gets.

Not that I haven't thought, as I always do in such situations, that as near perfect as it is, one day I will come back and the perfection will be complete. It used to be that I thought you were the missing piece. I was in some lovely place without you and I would think: one day I must come back with you and then . . .

But then I found you thought the same thing. By which I

mean, *we* thought the same thing when we were in some lovely place *together*. Ghent, was it? The view of St. Michael's Bridge at night? We were hand in hand, a little drunk, a little horny, as happy as we had ever been and ever would be, and one of us said it. One day we must come back : . .

And don't think I am going to fall into the trap of thinking the moment was perfect then if only we had known it.

As good as it gets is as good as it gets. It doesn't get any better than that.

The first indication is the merest theoretical mercury drop. Point something of a degree, if that. Then not so much a wind, as a hint of one. A forewarning. Of herald clouds, grey rags in the blue wash. Then squadrons hurtling in. And before you know it, a wipe-out of sun and sky. A blanketing of grey. That ominous atmosphere. That mood-swing. That temperature crash. Wait for it . . . the first full, fat drop. Plop. Plop . . . plop, plop, plop. Then a hammering. An absolute hammering. Buckets full of nails hurled at tin rooftops. Dry gutters thrashing and splashing, desperate for breath, as the rain is sucked down drainpipes into gurgling drains and away. In an instant, the concrete footpaths down through the mountainside garden are in full sluice and spate. The whole complex is a water park. Flumes and chutes and half-pipes.

There's a water-sheet fountain effect around my balcony. Surround sight and sound. I am totally water-curtained on three sides. And out there the tranquil swimming-pool sea is now Stygian. Turbulent with sea monsters. One shudders at the thought of being out in it, as some fishing and tourist boats are. Shudders? Okay, more of a delicious shiver, as one looks out from one's dry prospect, with its precise configuration of pitches, overhangs and run-offs. Not a drop on the surfaces of the deck. All cosy and dry in here.

In the gardens, the bananas and palms and cannas are being

whipped about, but hey, they're in their plastic macs and cagoules. They're in their high-concept wet-weather wear. The raindrops positively bouncing off them. But how do the tissue-paper flowers and crêpe leaves, the tiny budkins and tinker-bells, withstand the onslaught, as they seem to do, shrinking from, but then perking up as the perking up as the sun—as it, just wait—peeps out again?

Back from the murderous black of the sea, the beach has been strafed and has run for cover into the rain-deafened beach bars. The beautiful people, the tanned and lovely, now standing, damp towels wrapped around shoulders, all ashiver, under the ragged palm-frond roof of the sand-floor verandah, with their plastic pints of Red Stripe and bags of slightly damp tortilla chips. Not what they paid for. Though there's cama-raderie in this run for it and this standing there and looking out on it.

It's really something, this electric one-act. In and out of here, like a flash mob of drama students. Rain, guys! Whip up a storm. Chuck the kitchen sink at it. And before they know what's hit 'em, it's a wrap.

But one moment. Didn't I mislay the son et lumière, the thunder and lightning effects? Not necessarily. As often as not these rain dramas come and go without the full Wagnerian fire-works. They're more Debussyan in build-up, tumult and slow diminuendo. Less a work in heavy oils, more in watercolours.

Within minutes the storm has squalled through, raced out to sea, and there's a washing-on-the-line freshness and restora-tion in the air. Just some drip-drying to be done. And already the heat is returning, creeping out from under sodden bushes and stoking the brick oven. There is a return of insect static and bird twitter. Those delicate flowers are spangled with rain-drops, pearl-centred, clinging fingertip to their upturned cups and bead lines.

Down on the beach I can see bathers flagging the damp

sand with bright towels. It/they will be sun-baked in seconds. Pastel sarongs are being paraded again on the arms of the hawkers, hawkers with dozens of pairs of cheap sunglasses on their head—and half a dozen straw hats. The horizon line is back, freshly drawn. It will sharpen up soon. As I speak, you would never know. It is the brochure shot out there. The screen saver. The only evidence of the downpour—not visible from here—great red mud puddles in the potholed roads. The four-wheelers will be dropping into first, climbing in and out of the craters, back into second and away. Up the hill, and around the headland. On to the next resort.

All is somnolence again. The immense ennui of late afternoon in the tropics. (Or for that matter, at any latitude.) But the next big show will be along soon: the sunset experience. I jest, but one does get the sense sometimes that these are all staged as part of the tropical paradise package.

I will have that swim shortly. Once mid-morning and then again late afternoon has been my schedule over these first three days. You could call it a routine. It is certainly the life. One other thing while I am at it. I am pleased to say I remembered to bring my binoculars. The ones you bought me for my fifty-fifth. Five hundred pounds they cost, as you were keen to remind me. And why exactly did I want them? I mentioned stained glass at the time, but the other thing was birdwatching. Not the greatest interest of mine, I will admit, but occasionally in Urke and now here.

Closest to me—and granted, there's no need for the binoculars with them—are the hummingbirds. The gardens and balconies are festooned with feeders full of sugar water at which the hummers dart and dock, a kinetic blur of needle-point beak, pin-boned wing and iridescent coat. They are almost bumblebee tiny. Sometimes crested, sometimes fluffy-headed, sometimes more slicked back. All colours.

There are plenty of other bird types—flycatchers, bee-eaters, kingfishers. I am not too precise on the names and species, though there is a bird guide in the room which I consult from time to time. This is where the binoculars come into their own. It is immensely pleasing—and it centres the mind nicely—to bring a bird one has spotted into sharp focus, to hold it still, observe its tics and tiny mannerisms.

And out in the bay, endlessly circling the fishing boats and catamarans, coasting on the thermals, are pelicans and kites and other seabirds. I say endlessly circling: every now and again they hang on a breath of hot air and then plunge—at knifepoint—on a perfect vertical into the waves. The dives are not deep. Or at least, the diver surfaces quickly. Almost at once, they are bobbing on top. A shake of the head. One senses an air of bafflement, even embarrassment. "I could have sworn . . . " They must spear a fish occasionally, I suppose. Or snag or scoop it, whatever it is they do. But I haven't seen a kill yet. Perhaps I don't know what I am looking for.

Whose idea was this? Ellen Peters. She and Mike had been out here at Christmas, loved it and thought it would be a perfect place for some (in her Edinburgh accent) "R and R" after a few months snowbound in the Alps. I was in London for three days before I came out here, staying with Mike and Ellen at their house in Camden.

They organised a drinks party to mark "my achievement," which I suppose was kind of them. And I won't pretend I didn't enjoy the fuss and congratulation, even as I was making light of my actual contribution. But I was glad too when the last few people left, when Mike and I could "retire" to his study for a nightcap or two that we certainly didn't need. We carried on drinking into the early hours. Eventually Ellen put her head around the door. Mike had to be in work the following day.

I am drinking too much, of course I am. That must have been obvious since I don't know when. Did it affect my chairing of the talks? I don't believe so. Had that happened it would have been unforgivable, not to mention unprofessional. I perhaps didn't feel as fresh as I might have done at the start of the day's sessions. But those early-morning mountain walks generally cleared my head. That and a trusty ibu or two. A plastic bottle of them beside my bedside with a big glass of water. I functioned well enough, I am sure. Functioning being the *mot juste*, perhaps. I am not entirely sure what a functioning alcoholic is, but I am perhaps an example of one. And I trust, *high-*functioning. Though no doubt it varies day to day.

"A proper drink?" "A proper drunk, more like!" I suspect some of my team thought that. Indeed, I must once have overheard someone say it, as it is not one of mine. And goodness knows what the two delegations thought. A certain contempt, perhaps? Just as, let's face it, I felt contempt for their blatant abstinence. There were no complaints made, anyway. I did a good job, I am confident of that. I am a good man, that is the fact of the matter. If the worst that can be said about me is that "Behrends likes a drink," I can live with that. And the fact is that for all the good the counselling, the mindfulness, the meditation, the medication, the getting back to work, these peace talks, this talking to you . . . for all the good that all of this has done, I don't know where I would be without drink.

"Another?"

I am down to the largely ornamental piece of pineapple. I am not letting him have it, though. No, I'll have that. I pick it out with the pointy end of my paper-and-stick cocktail parasol and pop it in my mouth. This is how I like my fruit: drunk on rum.

"Please."

I have abandoned "Why not" or "Go on, then." There is no kidding my good friend the barman that I am even an iota reluctant. I am on my—what?—fourth since I arrived here? But what the hell! I am sat on a stool at the clifftop bar, the sun setting into the Caribbean, hummingbirds at the sugar water in silhouette. All of which can be appreciated without being inebriated, no doubt, but then I wouldn't know!

The barman whips away my glass. Pulls out a fresh one. He starts mixing. Throws those moves they do with the cocktail shaker. I do a little shimmy on my stool and have to reach out to steady myself. I will stop after this one. Have a bite to eat.

All the resort staff are done out in the most garish Hawaiian shirts. Bright red with yellow bananas. Is this not borderline racist? I wonder. The barman is damned if he's going to rise to it anyhow. It is probably over-the-border racist to suggest he could crack a watermelon smile if he wanted to, but no matter, because he doesn't. I don't know what the employment situation is on his island—pretty dire, I'd imagine—but this fellow isn't going to pretend he is lucky or happy to be mixing cocktails for pissed rich white folks. Good for him, I suppose.

It is with proper vehemence that he spears a virgin chunk of pineapple with a cocktail stick and drops it into my glass. He takes out a new parasol, opens it ever so daintily and balances it, more daintily still, on the rim of my glass. I will have to remove it to take my first sip, of course. A little stand-off results. How long can I last before succumbing? He's watching me. He's going about his business, cleaning and drying glasses, serving others, but he is definitely watching me.

I adjourn with my cocktail to a now vacant table. It is suddenly dark. A night light flickers in a glass ramekin. I will definitely make this my last.

I find I am weeping. No one notices. Here, as everywhere, I've seen that look on people's faces that says, "I know you, you're . . . " But where do you go with that knowledge? I'm not shunned exactly. Left in peace, more like. My privacy respected. But it's dark now anyway. No one can see me sitting here in the dark, weeping. Happy hour is over. I am so happy. And at the same time, so sad. A confluence of the two. And I miss you so, so much. This place, the warm perfume of the night air, the effect of all these rum punches. I've been drinking them since before lunch. Goodness knows how many . . .

This is the life, though. The good life. I have had such a good life, haven't I? I am so lucky. We were so lucky, weren't we? So happy. Life is so short. But at the same time, it goes on so, so long. It is not so much all the years that have gone, as all the ones that are left. All these years and years ahead of me. What am I going to do with myself? More days and nights like these, I suppose. Not a bad way to live. I have so much to be grateful for. To be alive, and here, in a place like this, on an evening like this. And at the age one longs to be, the age of acceptance, of accomplishments, the age one never achieves. I am quoting from Salter here. From memory. I have always wanted to use that quote. *Light Years*. I might reread that when I get home. Wherever that is.

And I have helped end a civil war, don't forget. I don't know that I did very much, but still. People have been saying it is the pinnacle of my career. Downhill from here, then?

Did I tell you I am getting a knighthood? Sir Edvard and . . .

If only you were sitting beside me. I mean, here, not at the investiture. That. Oh, forget that! You would be complaining about something. Too hot, too cool, the mosquitoes, your drink, that couple over there. You would be annoying me in some way. But making me laugh. I am laughing now just remembering. Through the tears, so to speak. I am still weeping.

Goodness knows why, but this memory has come to me. This new guy in your office. Young fellow. At some point he asks, "Does anyone want to hear a joke?" "Yes," you say. Cautiously. "Why does Noddy have a bell on his hat?" he asks. Nobody knows. "Because he's a cunt."

I remember distinctly you telling me this story. You had just come in from work. We were having a glass of wine at the island in our kitchen. In the house we loved so much. I was cooking that night. Something simple. "Imagine telling a joke like that just days after you started working somewhere," you said. The nerve of it. We were crying with laughter. Tears streaming down our faces.

This is when I miss you most. *Because he's a cunt.* Why is that so funny? Tears are streaming down my face. It is, though, isn't it? Or we thought so. "Perhaps we are just very bad people," you said. The idea appealed to you. It was good to be a bit bad, you thought. I so wish you were here. I don't really know what to do without you, that's the problem.

A good cry, though. A power of good, a good cry. It's a while since I've had one. And a good blow of the nose. A power of good, a good blow. My father, my mother. Both long dead. When was the last time I thought about them? Have I mentioned them at all? And a sister dead before I was born. Never talked about. To put it another way, I never asked. Not until very late. Another story. And your mother and father. And friends. And you. All dead.

I have many friends. I am so lucky. I have so much to look forward to. I so wish you were here. I know you aren't. I am talking to myself. Inside my head. Peace talks. Where would I be without peace talks?

"Another?"

The barman has appeared. What must he think of me? I smile. Shake my head. He smiles. No doubt there is sadness in his life. I feel most sad for him, for other people, for all the sadness in the world. My heart breaks to think of it. I am so lucky. So lonely.

I tap my trouser pocket to check I have my key. It is attached to a piece of wood. The name of my apartment has been carved into it.

I am in Golden Sunset.

Further Reading

You never liked me recommending books. And I can imagine you saying, *Look, I have just finished this one, don't start telling me what to read next.* But books have been referenced—the usual ragbag—and so I am risking it.

I remember you admitting to me once, years after we first met, that one of the things you most liked about me at the beginning was that I was so bookish. Bookish *and* good-looking. A man never forgets a thing like that.

Do you get to read at all? The thought that you certainly don't is just another thing that breaks my heart.

Baudelaire, Charles (1821–67), *Mon coeur mis à nu* (1887)

Broks, Paul (b. unknown), *The Darker the Night, the Brighter the Stars* (2018)

Cioran, E. M. (1911–95), *Des larmes et des saints* (1937)

Fukuyama, Francis (1952–), *The End of History and the Last Man* (1992)

Hikmet, Nasim (1902–63), *9–10 Poems* (1945), translated by Randy Blasing and Mutlu Konuk

Jenkins, Roy (1920–2003), *Gladstone* (1995)

Kravis, Nathan (b. unknown), *On the Couch: A Repressed History of the Analytic Couch from Plato to Freud* (2017)

Larkin, Philip (1922–85), "Aubade" (1977), included in *Collected Poems* (2003)

Mann, Thomas (1875–1955), *Der Zauberberg* (1924)

Montaigne, Michel de (1533–92), *Complete Works* (2003)

Ovid or Publius Ovidius Naso (43 BC–AD 17/18), *Metamorphoses* (circa AD 8)

Pascal, Blaise (1623–62), *Pensées* (1669)

Pinker, Steven (1954–), *The Better Angels of Our Nature: Why Violence Has Declined* (2011)

Proust, Marcel (1871–1922), *À la recherche du temps perdu* (1913–22)

Said, Edward (1935–2003), *Orientalism* (1978)

Salter, James (1925–2015), *Light Years* (1975)

The Noble Quran (609–32)

Updike, John (1932–2009), *Bech at Bay* (1968)

West, Rebecca (1892–1983), *Black Lamb and Grey Falcon* (1941)

Acknowledgements

I would like to thank my agents at United Agents, Caroline Dawnay and Sophie Scard, for sticking by me and for their frank, encouraging, and sound advice over the years.

Thank you also to Alexandra Pringle at Bloomsbury for taking on *Peace Talks* so enthusiastically. She, Sara Helen Binney and Allegra Le Fanu have been supportive and helpful in many ways.

Sarah-Jane Forder was scrupulous with her copy edits and judicious with her comments—and then floored me by adding, right at the end of the manuscript, the most beautiful comment about *Peace Talks*. I was immensely touched by her thoughtfulness.

I am a solitary and single-minded writer and generally do not share my work in progress with anyone. However, my partner Claudia did occasionally get called to my desk in order to hear me read a "good bit" I had just finished. On most occasions, she had the grace to agree with my assessment.

About the Author

Tim Finch is a leading campaigner and writer on refugee and migrant issues. He formerly worked as a director for the Refugee Council, and has founded two charities, among them Sponsor Refugees. As well as working as a senior political journalist at the BBC, he has broadcast frequently on Channel 4, Al Jazeera and CNN. He is the author of two novels, *The House of Journalists* (FSG, 2013), and *Peace Talks* (Europa, 2020).